Eulogy

Second Edition

Eulogy

Second Edition

A.R. Perkins

TATE PUBLISHING
AND ENTERPRISES, LLC

Published by Tate Publishing & Enterprises, LLC
127 E. Trade Center Terrace | Mustang, Oklahoma 73064 USA
1.888.361.9473 | www.tatepublishing.com

Tate Publishing is committed to excellence in the publishing industry. The company reflects the philosophy established by the founders, based on Psalm 68:11,
"The Lord gave the word and great was the company of those who published it."

Published in the United States of America

ISBN: 978-1-63063-579-4
1. Fiction / Religious
2. Fiction / Historical
13.11.14

For my soul mate, without your inspiration, this creation would not exist.

Phases

Artwork by: Taylor G. Murray

"For we know in part and we prophesy in part, but when I was a child, I talked as a child, I thought like a child. When I became a man, I put childish ways behind me. Now we see but a poor reflection as in a mirror; then we shall know fully, even as I am fully known."   - Corinthians 13: 9-12

Epilogue

The moment I saw you in the field, I knew you were a treasure. I saw honesty, devotion, and kindness. As I grew to know you, though, I was in awe of your strength. You are the anchor that has kept me from drifting off course. You are the pedestal that has encouraged me through the loss of my family and home. You are the diamond that could not be crushed by the boulders thrown our way. I love you and I cherish you more than any physical thing. I will devote my life to being with you on every level of love- may we grow together in mind, body, and soul.

-Oriana's Vows

Rome

Augustus Caesar initiated Pax Romana. The lust for power had receded and the noble emperor delegated appropriately to trusted government officials. Here, I find peace: a sense of completeness. Though, nostalgia often drifts me to my farm a lifetime away.

Our home was simple- mud and straw held bamboo timbers together. Woven grass sheltered us from the sparse rainstorms. The floor, composed of eroded sandstone slates bonded in the same simple material, was lacquered with mud cement so as not to scrape the soles.

The front door opened to the living space. A tiny love seat, constructed of the tedious weaving and bamboo, sat along the wall adjacent the door. A waist-high silver marble sundial stood in the heart of a multi-colored floral rug. The Burman satisfaction to her hobby lay warmly on the slate in front of the seating place.

Two bamboo chairs sat at our sycamore table. Oriana helped weave the backings. The kitchen

Eulogy

was separated from the room we dined in by sycamore cabinetry. The same floor slate covered the counter tops.

In the only separate room from the open floor plan laid the same wood material-made bed frame. We stuffed sewn clothing and rags with dove feathers and straw to sleep on. Another indulgence Oriana could not be denied was her worship of Diana: shelves and side tables strewn with her likeness throughout the crowded bedroom. One entrance and exit led to the bed. The soothing incense enveloped my senses every night as we slept.

My Oriana would buy candles at the local market place and intricate them about the meager dwelling. Every week, she would surprise me with another decor. She would buy wool place mats and matching dishes. Laughing quietly to myself, I would notice her scramble to display them as I came home after guarding Port Capena.

I dreamt that night of the golden haze of wheat fields. I grazed my hands spread across the tall florets. I walked towards the bordering forest.

A.R. Perkins

Light peaked through the canopy like tiny stars nestled there. Her eyes still bright and blue glistened in the muddled shadow. Her fawn colored hands folded to match her shy expression. She eased out into the sunlight and her lashes squinted onto her perfect eyebrows. Her hair reminded me of autumn leaves shimmering bronze, gold, and wheat brown. Two flower-petal lips opened as if to speak to me.

"Boy! Where are you, Boy?" My father's voice interjected the meeting.

I felt cement steady my knees that were before very flimsy. My head turned toward his voice, but my eyes could not. Then, the doe ran through the shadow. I felt my arm jerk.

"Boy! Didn't you hear me! Go get the sharp-sickle," he yelled down at me.

"Yes, Sir," embarrassed, I rushed to obey.

Any opportunity I had thereafter, I would run past my father's gaze and wait by the forest in hopes I would see her again. Her beauty intoxicated my memories. The magnetism seemed so natural and I could not be without the polar side of me.

II

Eulogy

Soon after, I was found wandering the forest by a band of stray contubernium. Their missing colleague would subject them all to flogging. That was the way of it in those days, heartless and goal minded for themselves.

Their laws subjected others to suffering: innocent and guilty alike. They found me sauntering casually without awareness, only dew-eyed toward my obsession. The jolt of the possession woke me abruptly.

I did not have the mind to fight or call out. They bound my hands with leather and gagged me with a torn piece of the dead colleague's tunic. The wool absorbed what little liquid remained on my tongue. My lips soon bled with their stucco texture. Two of the stouter men carefully hoisted the deceased onto the spare horse and tied me to the stirrup with a braided leather belt. The horse was then pulled by the bridle along-side the lesser ranking soldier.

"That Idiot, what possessed him to climb that tree?" one lamented.

"Well, I guess he was trying to get a better view

III

over the wheat field," another explained. "I hate being lost. Now we'll never find our way back to the Century."

"No, wait, there's a clearing. What luck, Mercury is surely on our side in this quest," he exclaimed.

"Look, there's a village," noticed a third.

"Well, let's get to work, boys. Surely we'll find enough to eat to take back to the Century, and we might even find a few other things of interest," the leader professed darkly, winking.

The group mounted their horses and raised their swords in a unison tribal yell. The front six charged towards the village. The last one trotted quickly as I fought my weary legs to keep up.

"Hurry, boy! We're going to miss the fun," he growled at me.

He must have grown tired of my incapacity to keep up with his the horse. I found myself hurled horizontal, nearly swallowing the bloody gag as my gut was punched abruptly by the turf. My skin burned as the blades ripped it apart; knees finding every twig and pebble as they were catapulted into

Eulogy

them. Suddenly, my body twirled around. The shock of the stop pulled the muscles under my right arm. I could have braced for the impact if I wasn't so distracted by the urge not to choke myself. The lesser ranking soldier dismounted and took the tunic scrap out of my mouth.

"Sorry 'bout that, but I did tell you to keep up," he said, squeezing the lamb's belly he carried of fermented wine into my mouth.

"So, how old are you kid?"

I glared at him, silently for a long moment. Then- I winced at the new burn on my face.

"I asked you a question! You're going to have to get used to following orders now! Your age, Soldier," he grunted authoritatively.

"F- fo- fourteen, sir," I was still choking on the remains of parched wool.

I was not afraid, only angry. The defiance was short-lived and rather unnecessary by this point. The sadness overwhelmed my mind, wondering to thoughts of the girl in the forest. Would I ever see her again? During this confrontation with the purely egotistical and overbearing lesser ranked

A.R. Perkins

officer, the others had already captured several women, burned their straw makeshift shacks, and were packing up their booty in bed sheets.

"Are you finally here? We started without you. Send over the pack horse," the leader ordered.

The women were bound with belts as I was. Rope was linking them in a line. This dwelling place was so tiny; they only found five to capture. My eyes scanned them. All of them dressed in brown deer skin hides and crying quietly.

"Let me go! Please . . . let me go!" I heard from behind a pile of rubble that was once a fine place of worship.

"You're coming with us, pretty one," one directed her forcibly.

"I found this one praying 'no one would find' her to Diana," he said to the leader.

"Seems like the goddess wants your virtue to be left to us," he roared laughter at her.

"NO!" I yelled, "not her, please!"

I started to cry. I fell to my knees and pleaded to my captures.

"I vow my service to Rome and to your roman

VI

Eulogy

gods if you do not harm her. Let her be in my charge, I beg you! She is my Siren, my Armenian Field. I swear to you, kill me or you will find death swiftly."

My heart fell in my stomach and raced wildly. I tasted the salt water dripping down my mud-stained cheeks. They all stared at me, silent and wide-eyed. I knew they would do as they wished with us. We all turned to face the tall dark haired and eyed man.

After ages passed, he looked down, then at her, then at me. I felt the nerves in my shoulders and neck become numb. His eyes stern, then glistened with humor.

"Son," he said in a soothing calm voice, "I have a family myself. I haven't seen my wife in quite some time. But, since, you have such an attachment to this little fawn; I can understand your plight. I, too, found my love in such circumstances as this. I, though, did do as you promise to do. The empire is changing from the brutality it once was. Even Cleopatra herself, used her wondrous beauty to ensnare the Emperor *and* a Senator's love," he laughed lightly.

VII

He strolled with purpose toward her and bowed, "Dear one," taking her bound hands, "would you decline the offer this enchanted slave requests?"

Her head jumped off her shoulders, her brilliant teeth showing as her diamond blue eyes glistened at his with gratitude.

"Then go to him and no one will lay a finger on you."

He removed a charred leaf from her autumn colored hair.

I woke to the sunlight, my dream reality as Oriana lay at my side. Her steady breathing moved her auburn back and shoulders. Her locks glistening as the sun escaped through the sheer pearl colored curtain. The Armenian Field was nothing compared to every moment I spent with her.

To be past that time in my life that I dreamed of was a blessing. Sighing as I stared at her, I forced myself up and uniformed my body with ease and reluctance. I maneuvered my way around her

Eulogy

dainty feet to the exit. The sundial that stood beneath the skylight displayed seven-thirty. I went to the kitchen and opened the cabinet to find some unleavened bread and cheese. I opened the bottle of wine Oriana bought yesterday on her excursion. I filled a green ceramic bowl and sat in one of the bamboo chairs to eat quietly.

Startled, I rushed to answer a knock at the door: Oriana rustled and sighed-annoyed at the noise. I forgot to close the door silently behind me. I crept quickly and did so, then hustled to the door to answer, still full-mouthed. Leander was there to walk me to Port Capena. He helped me guard it on the other side of the great city wall.

"Hey," yelling robustly. "How's my stallion this morning?"

"Shhh!" I glared at him. "Oriana is still sleeping," I whispered.

Quieter than before, Leander said, "Oh! Sorry, sorry, she must be tuckered out from all those baby making attempts," he jostled my arm as he said it. I only rolled my eyes at him.

"After ten years of 'knowing' her, you'd think

IX

you'd done something by now!"

We walked to our station as he razzed some more on my manhood. He could not understand my love for Oriana, I did not care if we had a baby or not. Sure, a tiny copy of us would be nice, with her eyes and my strong will, but it would not cease or emphasize how I felt for her.

We took to our station, spear in hand, face forward, and open eared, I stood throughout the length of the day until the sun set over one of the seven mountains. Listening to the travelers as they passed was my favorite part of the job.

"Have you heard of the Galilean," one scruffy looking traveler asked.

"Yes, Oh yes! My daughter was getting married and we ran out of wine. He turned the barrels of water into barrels to wine! At least that is what I hear. I will miss my daughter sorely and I got a little over-zealous in the festivities," he laugh shamefully and blushed his plump face.

"After he healed my daughter's leprosy, I followed him to the mountain and heard him speak. He fed us all on five loaves of bread and two fish.

X

Eulogy

We sat all day and his words gave me so much peace and hope, my insides leaped at the words. They felt like music to my longing soul!"

This man's face brightened as he spoke, his eyes wide and glistening with emotion. Such craziness! How could a man do these things unless he was a god or a magician? I cared not of what they believed, only that they would believe such lies. I laughed under my breath and shook my head as they spoke. Gossip is so funny sometimes. As time passed, another passer-by spoke of the Galilean.

A woman shared, "I heard, as he walked through the streets of Capernaum, he cried 'who touched me!' and a blind man shouted, 'I can see!' He ran to Herod's wall and shouted up to the guards of the miracle."

"Yes, it happened. I was there and led the man myself to be healed. I heard the Galilean could do such things. The man he healed was my father," a man replied.

"Really, it's true? You must be crazy!"

"He's my father. He's been blind since his

wretched life came into this world."

"Well, if you profess that it be true after you know the man, I believe you. Then . . . I must find this man; my son is lame at the knees and never knew how to walk. Could you imagine, wishing and hoping to expect your child to take his first steps, and never see that day come?" Her voice cracked a bit, "He is twenty now."

"He makes usual rounds though out this empire, spreading his word to the known world. I heard him say to one of his followers that he would be in Jerusalem soon. I think that is his birth place."

"That is so far to take my son," she shook her head in despair.

"I will assist in making arrangements for you. Let us go to the stable. We will find a good mule and a wagon to load him in. Then we will go to the port and..."

Their voices faded as they walked toward their newly planned destinations.

The other sects were made to adopt our views by Augustus to keep the peace. Inwardly, they loathed us and wore their masks well enough. Laws

Eulogy

were the only reason for their discretion. It was easy to feel peaceful as a Roman. But with this magician, the rebelliousness bled through their pores and hope in change was dangerous. Their gossip filled the air with the stench of it. Why would our beloved god of war cause this? Was Augustus' time of peace so boring to his wrathful nature? None of these gossipers were of Latin decent. Their dialect varied and muddled. Traveling abroad taught me the fluency of their races. One of the perks of the job and an asset as a guard of this widely utilized gate.

Pensive confusion rattled my brain. Who was this man that caused such interest? How could these things be true? Why would Gaia create such a person to be born in times such as this? After the Punic Wars and constant feuding receded, now at the time of peace? Perhaps it wasn't Gaia at all. I wondered inquisitively about the dissension in the air as they spoke of this man. They talked very low in the vicinity of who they believed 'pagans.' It had to be Mars at work here.

"Leander," I inquired.

A.R. Perkins

"Yes, my friend?"

"Can you hold the fort down for a bit? I need to ask the Praefectus for a favor."

"Sure, sure, go ahead . . . if you can find him." Leander scoffed and held his mouth.

"Thank you, my friend, I won't be long. I know just where to find him." I smiled smugly.

I followed down the street and turned into the thermae. There he was, being adorned by woman feeding him grapes and offensive cheese. These bath houses were made for this, an escape from the hardships of the Roman life. I laughed to myself often about how hard a leader of the Roman legion could possibly be now. I bowed my head to the floor and entered gingerly and respectfully, trying not to stare at his enormous and exposed pale abdomen. He laughed joyously at his spoiled experience. I cleared my throat and apologized for the interference, my head still bowed genuflecting.

"Yes, what is it! I should have you flogged for such insolence?"

"Sire, again, I apologize for my intrusion. It is quite difficult to find you when you are not

Eulogy

indisposed. You are such a busy man with many responsibilities," I stated earnestly without cause to offend.

"Get on with it then, Son," he yelled while waving his muses away.

"I wish to seek council with King Herod, my lord. I have been hearing much gossip at Port Capena and it concerns me."

"Go on . . ." he perked up with interest, "what sort of gossip?"

"Well, sire, they talk of a Galilean. They say he heals the lame and does all sorts of magic. Surely, he could have no more power that a god, and yet, as they speak of him, they are in awe and believe what they hear. With the knowledge I have in my travels and the fluency of other tongues, I have discerned that this may be a potential threat to our peaceful existence. I wish to speak to Herod and inform him of this man, so that he can find him and take correct action before he becomes a major problem."

"Hmmm. . ." he became thoughtful and rubbed his burly white chin, "you may have a valid point there." He pointed at me after a moment, and said

"I tell you what, instead of going to King Herod with this, let me run this by the Senate. I would not want my prize soldier to become drawn-and-quartered for random gossip's sake. Herod's lust for blood is more than a Spartan's."

"Yes, your honor. I understand."

I rose from my kneeled stance and backed away towards the exit, never raising my head until I found the archway.

"How did your meeting go?" Leander laughed. "Was his old skin fig-like enough for you?"

"Fine, Leander," eye rolling was a regular trait I acquired when we conversed.

"The sun is almost touching the mount. I hope our replacements come early. I need a trip to the thermae myself," hands on his lumbar, he rotated his stance.

"I just can't wait to see what trifles my Oriana has decided to surprise me with today," I smiled at him.

"You really love her, huh," he asked confused.

"You have no idea friend. Maybe someday, a passer-by will strike your fancy," I nudged my arm

Eulogy

with an elbow in his direction.

"O! No, no, no, not for me. I'll be single for life, Brother," his head shook shocked by the thought. "I do not want a chain on my fancy. There's too much of me to go around," arms spread, he laughed loudly.

The replacements came with orders for a month from now. Leander was to go half the world away to Mesopotamia. I was to guard Pontius Pilate in Jerusalem. There was a bonus for travel expenses and two addresses at the bottom of the order. I looked at the orders in wonder. I did not question the reasoning. I learned a long time ago, fighting was only when our livelihood was at risk.

"Well shall we go, my friend" Leander asked.

"Will you miss me, you old softy?" I jumped up and tousled his hair.

"Na, I'll be fine, this stallion," beating his chest, "cannot be stabled remember," he punched my shoulder with jostling force.

Perhaps, the discussion I had with the Praefectus had caused the decision for change. At any rate, it was definitely a step up from guarding a gate.

XVII

A.R. Perkins

Pontius Pilate was an important man. He was the Governor of Judea. Would this be my opportunity to discuss my concerns, or had the Praefectus done that already? These questions riddled me, but not an effect of defiance.

Leander squawked on about his excitement at his travel arrangements while I pondered. We arrived at my tiny dwelling.

"Hey, I've been jabbering while you haven't said a word. Are you okay with this, me leaving? Since we are going in the same direction, we should make travel arrangements together. It will be so wonderful to have a short sabbatical."

"Oh, of course I am friend. It's the way of things. I will see you tomorrow," he took my hand and drew my chest to his.

As every day at the end of the day, he stated, "Later, brother, if not soon, in death," and patted my shoulder under his dish sized palm.

Oriana ran towards the door to greet me. As I walked through the door, I noticed this week was purple. Also, there was a new addition to our abode, something she rarely bought on her outings.

Eulogy

There on a new side table, sitting beside our living area's seating stood a mid-sized vase. The picture on it was of Orion, the hunter. I picked up the vase rotating it, right to left. Orion was beside a lion, elevated on his back paws in a defensive attack mode, and a giant scorpion, stinger facing the hunter- all were etched in black on the tan marbleized background.

"I bought it for you, My Love," Oriana embellished, "it reminds me of you. Your sun sign is in Scorpio, your moon is in Leo, and you are my warrior. Your keen senses strike those that would harm me and your heart is that of a lion. As I sit in this house, I think of you and this will help me to not be so sad," she said pouting.

"Well, I'm home now, my little Siren. How could I stay away from the song you play at my heart strings?"

She smiled the familiar smile she showed to the leader of the contubernium so many lifetimes ago.

"I have some great news for us," I handed her the orders given to me by the Praefectus' messengers.

XIX

A.R. Perkins

She read them and gaped, wide-eyed up at me, "The Governor?" She shook her head in disbelief. No sadness or delight lit her expression, only absentminded alertness.

I grazed her forearms with comforting explanation, "Things will be better for us. It's a promotion of sorts. I spoke with the Praefectus today about a problem I'd noticed and he must have been impressed with my keen senses."

Then she smiled understanding, "See, like a scorpion, you sense things about you," she stated matter-of-factly pointing toward me. She wrapped her slender arms around my thick shoulders and nuzzled her nose into my chest, "I am so proud of you. Your promises never stop being fulfilled."

Then grazing her finger tips down the inside of my arm and twining her fingers into mine led me to the kitchen, "Come see what I bought for dinner."

We sat in our homespun furniture and began to eat from our regal colored dining ware,

"You know, Oriana, this is a good thing for us, but it is also a big change. We have a lot of planning to do, and packing, and the travel time will

Eulogy

be considerable."

She put her finger to my mouth and said, "Let us be in our moment right now, great protector."

Her eyes soothed my anxious ones instantly. We ate in silence, hands touching and stared lovingly at each other.

After our meal of herbs, flat bread, and figs, I went to the side table in the bedroom by the door and lifted a loose slate stone under the left front leg. I removed my cedar wood box that lay under the foundation.

Coming out, box in hand, "Oriana? I hate to intrude."

She came to me and noticed the box, "Well then shoo, shoo away silly, I'll get it," Oriana playfully pushed me out the door.

I left and closed the door, after a moment she came out with her own cedar wood box.

"It will take all of our money to set up the travel arrangements," I said.

"I understand. It will be so odd to be away from Rome after living here for so long. Will it be nice in Judea?" Her lips curled upward on one side and

XXI

the same eye squinted at her inquisition.

Awakened from a nonchalant state, I knew I must warn her. She: so naive and frail, sheltered by one belief, one life, one mind set. She: who took care of our home with such excitement and care, who knew nothing of war, murder, and different ways. I loved her for her lack of knowledge in such things. She was my solace from all that soldiering intruded upon my psyche. My eyes shot sternly at hers as I gripped her shoulders strongly.

Breathing and staring intently into her fathomless eyes, I beseeched, "We must be careful there, my love. You cannot profess to Diana with such fervor as you do here. Their religion is strange and many are killed for any defiance. Religion and law are one in the same there. Law is exercised by the people through rioting. Pontius Pilot recently arrived there to bring about order, since the King Herod could not. It is a hard time to be stationed there now, but as long as we keep to ourselves and watch what we say, we should be fine. Do you understand?"

Her chin moved solemnly upward once and then

Eulogy

to her neck again, her eyes never returning mine.

"I do not say this to scare you, Oriana, but I am not sure how far away from you I will be. When we first arrive, we must tour the landscape a bit. I do not want you to go to the marketplace until I know you are safe okay?"

She looked up at me angrily, her diamonds eyes fumed with the wrath of the sea. I breathed in hesitation and regret for the need of my words.

"How can you expect me not to be terrified, when you obviously are?"

Now I'd done it. Stripping her from her only excitement was a bad idea. She became like a spoiled princess after executing her lame horse.

"Just, what am I supposed to do?! You will be gone all the time while I sit in a house I am unfamiliar with" I put my finger over her mouth this time, my green and amber eyes calmed her instantly.

"Shhh!" I moved my hand to cradle her head and kissed her pursed petal mouth. "I only say this to protect you, my raging whirlwind. You are strong as the sea, but just as impossible to tame."

XXIII

A.R. Perkins

Still a bit unsettled, but smiling at me lovingly, she grabbed my waist and squeezing again whispered, "You have tamed me, my love."

I pulled her hips away from my body and looked at her, holding her childlike jawbone in my massive hand.

"I know, limbo is a terrible place, but as we float on the river Styx awaiting the judgment to Hades or the Armenian Fields, we must be patient. Do not fall into the river of blood without my oars to guide you. Promise me this, Oriana" I pleaded earnestly.

"Yes, my love, always. Your oars have never steered me wrong."

We embraced for a long while taking in the features of the home we built together.

XXIV

"For I know the plans I have for you, plans to prosper you and not to harm you, plans to give you hope and a future." - Jeremiah 29:11

Jerusalem

Leander knocked at the door. I was not as startled this time as I ate the leftovers from last night's supper. I hurried to answer it.

"You ready?" he whispered.

"No, you're early, friend. I wanted Oriana to come with us this morning. She's not used to being out of her element. I think being a part of the travel plans would be good for her."

"Well, go get her up then, I tried some of that Turkish coffee grounds this morning and my legs feel like they are going to run away from me."

"Turkish coffee . . . do you have any left? Do you have it with you?"

"Sure, sure," he handed me a red bag with a silk brown string tie surrounding it closed.

I smiled winking at him. Catching on, he snickered as we went inside and diabolically made the brew noiselessly.

"What's that wonderful smell?"

Oriana stretched and came out leaning against the door frame with nothing on. We stared at her for a moment. No matter how long I'd seen her

Eulogy

that way, she still affected me as she would any other man that had never seen it before. Reality woke us both up, from the moment. I realized Leander was staring, Leander realizing that I realized he was staring.

"Oh," Leander breathed loudly in his burley voice as he turned around.

Oriana, not familiar with the voice in her unsteady state, opened her eyes and screamed as her door shut.

"Oriana," I tapped on her door, "put something on and come out here. It's okay. Leander is my best friend, he will not remember by the time you come out here. *Will you, Leander?*" I gritted my teeth at him.

"No, I won't, what were we talking about again?" he winked. "I didn't even see anything anyways. I was too busy spilling the coffee."

"Coffee," Oriana frilled.

She was out quickly, her embarrassment subsided. I pulled the love seat over to the dining table and all three of us sat there, Oriana and me in the love seat and Leander in one of the chairs across from us.

"Are you going to tell her," Leander hinted, "or should I?"

"Oh, yes! Oriana, we would like you to accompany us as we plan the trip and spend some of our money. You can pick out your own horse and travel clothing."

Her face, bright as the sun, jerked her coffee before she could place it on the table to embrace me. She danced in her seat, wiggling her feet.

"I guess the coffee's gotten to her too," Leander joked looking at the new stains on my tunic.

"Oh it's just so wonderful, one huge shopping trip before a month on a boat away from my marketplace. I will even get to tell my vendors good bye. I will go get proper immediately."

She chugged her coffee like a man drinking at a brothel and ran to the bedroom. Leander and I put our bowls on the counter and waited.

After a while, "Shoo, I am *never* getting married," Leander said impatiently.

"Oriana, what do you have to improve on? You are perfect the way you are," I complimented. "Now come on, Leander is getting antsy."

Eulogy

Leander rolled his eyes.

"What?" I was perturbed.

"Do you always have to treat her that way to get *your* way? Like I said, no chain for my fancy, *No. . . Thank. . . You!*"

"I've grown accustomed to what she likes. Marriage takes patience and team work," I explained. "Besides, we saved each other a long time ago, since the moment I saw her. If I hadn't met her, I'd still be on that retched farm, and Zeus only knows where she'd be, probably dead."

"Humph! Well it's just not for me."

A few more moments later, she was dressed in a white lace eyelet gown. Her hair braided from crown to waist. Diamond cascade like earrings draped to her neck. Her hair was fastened with a silk white ribbon and a peacock feather shaft interwoven in the ribbon adorned the makeshift barrette. She latticed her feet in white moccasins. No matter how much we had, she always knew how to frugally create an impression.

The cedar boxes were our savings for when we bought another house. These hopes were derivative on whether or not Oriana would bear a child. Since,

A.R. Perkins

I would receive a bonus, half from the Praefectus, half from the Governor when I reported for duty, and a house, we could afford to splurge a bit of our savings. I retrieved the boxes and the three of us stepped out the door. We traveled west on Vicus Censori toward the port. While Leander and I spoke with the man at the dock, Oriana would visit the stable to pick out our horses.

"We'll be here unless you take a bit longer to find the best horses for us. If so, we will be at the Senate speaking with Praefectus. Hopefully, you can find some good ones. I know you have the best eye for these things," I informed Oriana as we walked away separately.

"I'll come find you if there's a need," she shouted to us after a short nod.

We set up the time perfectly with the sailor. He stated it would take six days to make it to Judea across the Mediterranean Sea, traveling around the toe and heal of Italy. We would leave in a week and that would give us eighteen days to travel to Jerusalem, find the home, adjust to our new city and settle in, before I reported for duty with the Governor. Jerusalem was a two day trek from the

Eulogy

coast. Two weeks was enough time to pack.

We then followed the street back across, past the stable, and towards the center of the city beyond the Forum. We climbed the huge steps up the hill to the Senate. We walked past the ionic columns and the marble silver stone. The floors showed our reflection as they were recently waxed. Small boys dressed in rags and dark mud-stained faces glared at us as we sauntered our travel born mud on their work. At the end of the hall, we turned left into the Praefectus' office.

"Hello, my boys!" he roared and opened his wide and gracious arms. "All is well I hope?"

"Yes, sir," we said, our heads bowed genuflecting.

"Come now, come now get up, I will not be seeing you to for a while and I do hope you enjoy your short time left in Rome."

We rose from our knees, our heads still bowed.

"Here, I know this is what you came for," He laid two envelopes on the table, each with our names on it.

"Spend it wisely," he eyed at Leander.

"Thank you, sir," we yelled strongly and

simultaneously.

Then we beat our right hand to our hearts and genuflected goodbye. We held our composure until we got half way down the hall. Leander and I skipped liked children punching each other in excitement and joy. Leander opened his envelope first. The envelopes were only statements signed and sealed by the Senate to take to the lamnia.

"Fifty thousand gold coins!" His eyes popped opened.

"Well you have a long way to go. It's a fair compensation for your trouble."

"Open yours," he suggested excitedly.

I opened the enveloped and peeked onto the statement. My eyes met his soberly.

"What? Are you disappointed? I'll go back and speak to him right now for you." He sauntered angrily down the hall back to our former destination.

"No, Wait!" I said.

"It's not a problem. I can talk to him for you."

"Look," I reluctantly turned the paper to show him the amount.

His eyes inflamed gradually. His reaction was

Eulogy

interrupted by a high pitched rumbling sound and a vibration of thick skin blowing echoes throughout the hall. We crept out of the shadow of the archway. Our eyes were blinded by a glow of white on white. Her arms spread holding two bridles. Her eyes closed her head high. Of course she would pick white, her dress matched it today.

"Hello, my princes. Your regal steeds await you. I got the big one is for you, Leander. He will do be a good pack horse. Roman horses are not near as fast as the ones in Mesopotamia. Yours, my stallion, is black and dark as your hair."

She had found wonderful and strong horses. Leander's was an auburn red-brown, with a white stripe from his forehead to his tail from underneath, and he was bigger than the other two. All of them were well fed with bright gentle eyes and not a hint of sloping in the spine. Oriana's saddle was white leather and the blanket beneath imprinted with green and purple peacock designs.

"Good job, my love. Didn't she do a good job, Leander?"

He was still angry and said nothing.

"Ok," I pulled him aside and spoke under my

breathe, "I understand that you are going farther than me and you are not getting a house in the bargain, nor a promotion, or any of that, but what is it you want me to do? I do not have the pull that you do, or thought you once had. Just because you thought you had a thing going with his daughter, does not mean anything. Things change here too quickly, Leander. I'm almost wishing that it would all end. The politics, the lies, the gossip, the torture, but we have to do what we have to do to survive. I will not put my family at risk for your neck!"

His eyes softened.

"Are we good, Leander?"

"We're good."

"Now stop acting like such a child. Oriana *did* buy you a fine horse."

"That she did, my friend."

"Well then, let us not mention this again. There is no need for jealousy among friends."

We walked back towards Oriana and mounted our newly acquired possessions. We walked them towards the lamnia, as we chatted about their names. Oriana initiated that conversation. We really didn't care too much about it and she would

Eulogy

pick them out anyway. I would wait for a proper time to tell Oriana about the purse, when Leander was not present to light up his temper again.

Oriana went into the lamnia with us and Leander collected his purse first, then walked back to Brutus bridled to the post outside. I showed her the slip just to see the look I knew she would give me. Nothing made me happier then to see her face shine like the sun with child-like glee: two-hundred and fifty thousand coins. She held the smaller bag, while I carried the two heftier ones.

It was a good thing I brought my sword with me. One would have to have one's own personal body guard with this much cash and I was just the one to defend it. We returned to Rosalba Eleron and Marcellus Sienna along with Leander and Brutus Maximus.

"So, Leander, you never told me what you are doing in Mesopotamia."

"Oh, guarding a gate."

"That's all?"

"Yes, that's all. I'm traveling half way across the world to guard a gate," he stated with such bitterness, I didn't press the issue.

We went back to our meager shack in silence and Leander said his good-byes, "If not tomorrow, then in death, brother."

"See you then, brother."

Oriana hugged him, "I hope you enjoy Brutus, Leander. Feed him an apple or two for me, okay?"

"Good night, sister, sleep well if you can."

We all laughed. Oriana could always lighten a mood simply by her presence.

"Well, Oriana, we have two weeks to pack. I know we haven't done this much, but here's the plan . . ."

One morning, becoming accustomed to the habits of this vacation, I woke when it was nearly afternoon. Oriana's eyes were open when I woke up, and lying beside me.

"I threw up," she said.

"Huh, you did what," I asked wiping the sleep from my eyes.

"I threw up."

"Well our diet hasn't changed that much. I hope

Eulogy

you didn't eat anything unusual while I was at work yesterday."

"No, my love, I don't think food poisoning is it. I saw the midwife today while you slept, and she confirmed that I am with child."

"Well, Oriana, this is wonderful news." I leaped from the bed and swung one of her statues of Diana around and kissed it. Then I took the statue, laid it beside her on her pillow, patting its head, and kissed Oriana full on her mouth for an age.

"Mmm, mmmm," she pushed my forehead, "it's wonderful that I threw up?"

"No, hun, don't you know what that means? You...we...are having a little one."

"I know that dear, but does this not ruin our plans?"

"No, Oriana, women travel with child all the time, even farther along than you will be. I promise I am not disappointed. We have waited so long for this: Praise, Diana!"

All the packing was done. With this news, I was glad of it. I saddled Marcellus and went to the carpenter to buy a wagon. It was not the largest or the smallest he had. Back at the abode, I started loading the carpet full of dishes Oriana had wrapped carefully and tied on both ends. I loaded the chairs and the table. The statues of Diana were packed under the table and wrapped in our mattress. We would buy a new one in Jerusalem. Oriana had torn it apart with this hope.

The bed frame laid on the living space and we had slept on the floor. I packed the bed frame next after disassembling it. The sundial would stay until our final day. The red dish ware was kept out for us to eat on. The basin also would stay as well as the love seat. Her towels made of Egyptian cotton were left out to place between the furniture for the tumultuous via. All seemed to be falling into place.

The next morning, Leander was waving at me through the kitchen window, "I see you already bought a wagon this morning."

"Yes, I was just so excited, I couldn't sleep in today. It *finally happened,* Leander. Oriana is with child. Is that not wonderful?!"

"Well, I guess that means you aren't worthless," he rolled with laughter and smiled at me.

I just smiled back at him.

"So, what's the plan today," Leander asked.

Eulogy

"We are going to get you a wagon and I'm going to buy Oriana an Egyptian duck down bed, like the one Cleopatra slept in. That's what she wants and I need it before I can pack the rest on the wagon."

We went through the busy marketplace, being jostled as people side-stepped our careful movements. A mule brayed as he was being pulled angrily by a man beside us. The vendors' voices rattled in random accents. I couldn't understand what brought Oriana here every week. It was nerve racking claustrophobia. We finally made it to the mattress and bedding vendor. He had the largest spot at the last aisle on the left. Leander bounced his seat on each bed to see if it was cozy enough. I found the mattress she wanted, paid the vendor twenty thousand coins, and Leander helped me lift it.

"Shoot, I forgot the wagon."

"Hey, you stay here while I go buy mine and I'll bring it back here."

"Ok...hey...what about your hors . . ."

He was already gone before I could finish.

Moments later, here he came back hauling the

A.R. Perkins

wagon behind him at top speed. Angry shoppers yelled at him as he barreled through. I eyed at him in bemusement and awe. We loaded the mattress into the wagon. I walked beside him as he lifted the front and we walked back to surprise Oriana. She wasn't awake yet. I lifted one end, he the other as we walked crab-like into the house. We placed it down quietly beside her on the bare bedroom floor. Leander lifted her awkward shoulders, I got her feet and he placed her on the mattress. She never interrupted her slumber.

I whispered, "You got any more of that coffee?"

"Yes, sir I do," He laughed quietly.

We made the coffee and after a few moments when the coffee brewed, we heard a scream and a loud THUMP!

"Oh, my god, Leander," we rushed to the bedroom.

"Are you okay, Oriana? You didn't hurt anything did you?"

I grabbed her up and brushed her hair from her face, eying her over for bruises.

"I didn't think I was in my own house. Is that coffee?"

Eulogy

We laughed.

"Yes, Oriana, you're sure you're okay?"

"Yes...yes, I'm fine, love. Thank you for this beautiful bed. I will enjoy my ride to Jerusalem," she pushed on it and stroked it lovingly. "You surely do know how to take care of us," she patted her belly with loving eyes.

"It wasn't cheap," Leander growled.

He still couldn't let it go.

"Here," I threw a pouch at him full of one thousand coins.

He caught it fumbling awkwardly.

"Thanks for the coffee, now *get out! Come back when you can learn to behave yourself.*"

    "Fine with me," and he left.

Leander didn't come back the next morning, or the morning after that. I wondered if he still wanted to ride with us. I went to his house and saw that all of his things were packed in his wagon and Brutus was outside tied to his hitching post. I knocked on his door. There was no answer.

"Leander, are you there?"

I knocked again, *"Leander!"*

"What!" He flung open the door.

We glared at each other and I walked away. He was obviously not over this.

"Hey," he interjected my stride, "see ya for our trip man. Sorry about my behavior."

I turned, "No, problem man, just please watch it around Oriana, okay. She doesn't need any more stress right now. It's hard enough for her with the traveling and all. She's afraid it will hurt the baby."

Softening his flaming glare, "I understand," Leander conceded.

The big day had arrived and I loaded the mattress, bed frame, side tables, and sundial gingerly around Oriana as she sat in the wagon. Rosalba was tied behind the wagon and Oriana rubbed her nose lovingly, patting the side of her neck as we traveled toward the port.

"This is so wonderful, love," Oriana said to me.

I just smiled and faced foreword. Oriana found her way to the boat while I loaded the freight. The captain welcomed us.

"My name is Peregrine." He spread his arms, twirling slowly around, "Welcome to my home!"

While Oriana overlooked the tattered vessel, I pulled Peregrine aside and discussed her condition.

Eulogy

I asked for quarters to accommodate her. He went over to her, took her hand, and kissed it as he bowed. This made her laugh and blush awkwardly.

"Come, my sweet, mermaid. Follow me."

He led us down the hallway to the sleeping quarters. It was rather large for the small boat.

"Is this your quarters, Peregrine?"

"No, no, I never sleep here. I'm only comfortable on my cot by the helm. I can't hear the sea spray as much down here, so I get too nervous to sleep. Besides, the lass needs a proper place to sleep, and the spare room adds to the appeal of the special price," he winked.

"Are there anymore rooms" Oriana asked.

"No, I have some hammocks in the cargo hold though."

"Poor, Leander," Oriana said.

I looked at her, shook my head, and whispered, "I would sleep down there with him but I don't want you alone up here with all these atrocious men, Oriana."

She looked up and nodded at me.

The walls were brown planks. The décor was filled with giant star fish and anchors. Fish net was used as a canopy for the bed.

"This is actually kind of nice," Oriana said.

She lay on the bed. She inhaled through her nose naturally a couple of times and then a few more times in short increments.

"Could you get the mattress, love?" She plugged her nose and said nasally, "This one kind of stinks."

I couldn't smell anything, but I did as requested and lugged the mattress from below. I set the other mattress in the closet, shutting the door. She opened the porthole to let some air in. Lying on her mattress again, she shut her eyes. I crept out and waited for Leander while she slept.

Marcellus and Rosalba were in the cargo hold along with everything else. I visited them and fed them an apple a piece for Oriana. I heard a deep clopping sound coming down the stairs. I looked there and saw Leander and Brutus.

"Come on you stupid beast! This animal, man, has the temperament of a mule."

"Oriana picked him well then, hey," I jostled his arm.

"Humph," Leander glared at the floor.

Eulogy

"What? It was just a *joke*. Don't tell me you are still mad."

"Actually, I'm not mad at *you* anymore," Leander explained. "I never really was. I'm thinking about going A-wall and coming to Jerusalem with you. I could dress up like all those people down there in their robes and blend right in."

I looked at his bright blue eyed, strawberry blond cropped hair, and two-hundred fifty pound freckled frame and couldn't hide my laughter.

"What?" Leander asked shocked at my indiscrete thoughts.

"Nothing, my friend, if you want to come to Jerusalem with us, you are welcome to, but what about the pay you received? Won't the empire come after you for the money?"

"I'll pay it back to them once I get on my feet. I will be fine."

"Well unfortunately, Leander, I cannot allow you to live with me. It would be like hiding a thief."

"Hmm . . . You do have a point there. I will go to Mesopotamia, give them back the money honorably, and resign. I think I would like to work in stone anyway. I have the build for it, don't you think?"

Laughing, I said, "Definitely, Leander, that's why you wouldn't blend in too well in Jerusalem. You and your clean shaven face, bright eyes and hair. You would stick out like a sore thumb."

He smiled the first smile in my direction I'd seen in days. He looked around at the ship in distaste.

"Hey, where's Oriana," Leander asked.

"She's sleeping."

"O," he paused for a moment. "Hey, I brought some fishing poles and bait . . . you wanta?"

"Yes, brother," we fished for a while and then turned in for bed.

The sea was calm throughout the trip. We made it to our destination two days early. Leander started to travel northeast to Mesopotamia as he promised. We promised to write, and when he got settled and resigned, he would come and settle down here with us.

Eulogy

This loyalty surprised me. He was more of an acquaintance that a real friend anyway. He was young; he had plenty of time to choose where and who he wanted to be. He may continue to be a soldier since he loved to travel. He may come to Jerusalem. He may even be better suited in Egypt working the fields or building the huge limestone monuments. He could do anything. I was committed and perfectly content. We were like day and night. Regardless of how he saw himself as one who lacked commitment and a vagabond who became bored with stationary scenery, this new development showed me that there was more to Leander than he let on.

One may think I would be nervous with him around my Oriana, but that's where trust came in. Not trust of Leander but for Oriana. A part of Leander exuded repulsion at the idea of her, because she loved commitment. She loved her life with me. None-the-less he as well as I knew of the story of the tiny boy who killed the giant warrior with a stone. It would not take much for my anger to do that and much more, but loyalty was not necessarily derivative upon fear, simply, character.

A.R. Perkins

Leander had helped me load our wagon and unload the horses. Oriana was already comfortably settled in as we traveled the trek to Jerusalem. The huge golden dome shone above all the other buildings as we were far from the entrance. Oriana "ooohed" and "ahhhed" at the beauty of all of it: new and glamorous for her sheltered eyes. Map vendors were settled at the gate. I bought one and found our new home.

"Oh my," Oriana's eyes were locked opened at the sight of it.

"Yes and I am stationed a few blocks away. They put us in the best part of town, away from the noise of the vendors and the homeless district."

The home was enormous. The porch and the columns were silver granite. The door was made of copper and gold. It was actually rather heavy. As we went in, the archways led to other rooms and the cathedral ceiling was painted with oil pictures of the gods: Prometheus was given fire, Hercules was strangle-holding the Nemean Lion, Cassiopeia in bondage, Arachnea weaving her rug in competition with Artemis, the three fates holding scissors to cut some poor souls life short. These images were also throughout the hallways. The walls were of the same silver marble. The cabinets were cedar. The flooring was white limestone. There were five spare rooms not including the kitchen, bathroom, and living space. I unloaded the wagon and took the horses and the wagon to the stable that came with the home.

"I have plenty of spare room to buy nice things now, but I still like our chairs and table," Oriana said.

"Whatever you like, Oriana."

"Oh, look a little stove and our sink is nicer here then the spout we had outside."

The stove was a cast iron rack with a griddle on top. The underneath allowed space for a fire. The sink had a water pump from out of the ground and a drain.

"There are a lot of nice changes, Oriana. I told you this would be good for us."

"Will you go to the marketplace with me when we get done here? I would like to add our own touches to this place."

"Yes, Oriana, we can go to the marketplace as much as you want until I report for duty. We have a good week and a half until then."

She enjoyed this but a slight anger hinted in the eyes. She bought black and white horse statues. They were waist high and she placed them outside on either side of the right and left columns at the top of the stairs. I bought a mask of the hydra and placed it in the dining space. The mask was entirely black with red eyes. In the vase Oriana bought for me, she placed peacock feathers and set it in the corner of the dining room. These decorations were just starters to the additions of our new home.

We were fatigued after touring the city, finding Pontius Pilate's place of residence and the place he worked. We had bought lunch and ate. An aura of peace flowed between us.

Then after the days of moving pains had accomplished, the big day had come.

"Remember, Oriana, don't go out today unless your with me," I shouted as I left.

She was cleaning the breakfast dishes when I kissed her goodbye. I followed the road until I reached Pontius Pilate's abode to report for duty. He stood and I saluted him. He motioned his hand to a plush seat and relaxed within his own.

Eulogy

"I hear you have a good ear and can speak many languages" Pontius said.

"Yes, sir, I have heard many disturbing things about 'The Galilean.'"

"I only know that he *is* becoming a nuisance to the Sanhedrin. They believe that he will cause rioting and dissension among the Jewish people"

"I know many people believe in him, sir. I see these rumors as a nuisance as well, because they bring too much question to the people about authority. A man should not have the powers of the gods. Our legislature is dependent on our culture and religion does not necessarily coincide. Law has stayed true with these beliefs and this man could threaten our kingdom," I explained.

"Very well said, colleague, are you aware that they call him their king? They see him as their lost messiah, coming to rescue them from evil times."

I became thoroughly confused and too loose with my tone in front of the stranger, my new supervisor.

"*King? Messiah? Evil times*???" Again, it was easy to feel peace as a Roman.

"Yes. So with your keen ear, you have been sent

here to assist us in trying to decipher the truth behind these rumors. We cannot simply act upon what we hear. We need to be able to find this man and hear it from his own mouth, before we can prosecute him for treason against the empire. Here's to your keen ear and talent."

He placed the other two hundred and fifty thousand slip in my hands. I beheld it inwardly acknowledging, this *was* the reason I was here.

"You will sit in this seat, unless there are visitors, then, you will stand beside me, as long as I am at this desk. When I leave you will stand at the front gate, until your shift is over. Keep your ears open on and off duty. Take trips to the market place for me, things of that nature. You will be my ears on this operation."

"And what happens after the operation is over, Sire," I beat my chest and looked at the wall as I asked this.

"If you do well, you will be my man-at-arms. You will receive seventy-five thousand coins a week."

"Thank you, sir, and what are my orders currently?"

Eulogy

"Have a seat."

I did as ordered, for the rest of the day, no visitors. Pontius did not chat a lot.

He only said, "Guard the gate," and he retired to his lunch.

I ate when I felt like it as I sat "guarding" him. This was very good pay for absolutely nothing. What on earth did he really need me for? True, Pontius was a very important man, in a very dangerous area, but Leander would be better at protecting him than I would. I was a minuscule five foot ten compared to Leander and only weighed one hundred and eighty pounds. I was not a light weight or heavy, but fit enough for the army. This Galilean must be someone of great interest for Rome to have gotten involved.

Then it hit me, regardless of the rumors, the senators already knew about the problem. It was a matter of secrecy. When I made mention of it to the Praefectus, it made them aware that the problem had spread to Rome even though this man rarely visited Rome and rarely took a vessel across the sea. He always traveled by foot. His words were spreading to all people and this was dangerous territory to the Romans. The Pax Romana was being threatened by the already violent nature and they knew the people would revolt if this defiance spread too quickly.

Was that all worth my enormous salary? Was this blood money? These things I thought about as the sun went down. This time, my shift ended as the blinding sunlight hit off the golden dome. About the same shift, another perk, this was good. I enjoyed spending time with Oriana in the marketplace, and I knew she would not want to wait long when I got home to go. I walked from the residence, speeding my steps as a neared our new single story home. I pushed the heavy door excitedly.

"Oriana," I shouted, "I'm home."

I looked in the kitchen and she was not there. She must be sleeping, I laughed to myself. I cracked opened the slowly, just enough to peek through. The bed was made and incense was smoldering streams in the breeze of the opened window. The sight of her meticulousness made me smile and glow inside. I paused there for only a moment and then moved about the house calmly,

Eulogy

searching. The home had not seemed as enormous as it did at that moment. After not locating her after glancing briefly in each room, I researched thoroughly to the closets: no Oriana. Panic set in my arms and spine. I stood in the living space confused. Then, seething, I bolted out the door.

I walked past the temple and across the bridge toward the marketplace. I was a head taller that the other people of Jerusalem. Oriana's short stature was hard to recognize but I knew her golden locks would stand out here like I did in my height. The woman here wore scarves on their heads and long dresses. Oriana usually dressed like a Greek goddess in one her many colored tunics, as was customary in Rome, and always braided her hair when it wasn't a special occasion. I walked past the Upper City district and still could not see her. Then I feared the worst and rushed to the Lower City. As I neared the separation of districts I heard the commotion.

"*IDOL WORSHIPER*!"

"Look how's she's dressed! *ADULTEROUS*!"

"She claimed Diana gave her the child in her bosom. *Stone her*!"

A.R. Perkins

No. No! NO! Hearing the thumps of the stones on body mass before they clinked to the ground, I ran through the crowd, pushing bystanders to the ground towards the clearing of the mass.

I drew my sword at the circle of accusers as another man drew back to hurl another stone. I swung and dismembered him before the rock could be hurled to her body again. Fearfully, it was too late, for Oriana lay on the ground. Her white tunic stained in dirt from the rocks and her own blood. Her golden locks crusted with the heinous scabs that had begun to form from her forehead. I stood there gazing at her, the accusers ran away at the sight of me in my uniform, sword flailing violently at them. The puddle of the accuser's blood grew as he lay in shock on the ground.

I heard the clank as my sword felt heavy in my numb limb. The shock of the concrete hit my knee caps as I dropped before my love.

"Just please me be okay! Just please, don't die. Don't leave me alone, here in this wicked place," I whispered as I cradled her in my arms. I smoothed her mangled hair from her face and rocked her. "Oriana? It will be okay, talk to me my love. Look

Eulogy

at me. LOOK AT ME!"

I urged her to breath, to use those flower petal lips that made me love her so long ago: to let me see her brilliant diamond eyes once more. Her eyes flickered opened and glazed in mine. Her perfect eyebrows creased with the exertion of it.

"O, Oriana, hi, I'm home, dear, I'm home."

"I want. . .ed to sur. . . surprise you. . . your. . . first . . . day. The vendor saw. . . I . . .

was . . . with child. I'm sorry, my love, I'm sorry," and she gave her last breath.

Numbness flowed everywhere but my chest. I felt like a remnant tearing apart across the thread from neck to bowels. My head pained with the choking back of tears. I refused to cry. Acceptance overwhelmed me, and I picked her up. Now, I was truly alone.

I put her body in the Pool of Bethesda by the Holy Temple. I bathed her and changed her in front of the onlookers. I scowled at them and growled as they stared.

A uniformed man came and took my elbow lightly and whispered close to my ear, "You're not allowed to do that, sir."

A.R. Perkins

I took my sword and ran him through. Bystanders screamed as his body flailed to the ground. My attention forgot his body was there. I washed off the sword in the fountain, sheathed it, and continued my work on Oriana's body. I carried her to our home. I pushed opened the door with the shoulder opposite her head, and laid her in her bed. I sat down on the floor beside her, back resting against the frame. The numbness returned and the torn remnant fell to the floor inside me. I stared for a long time at the ground. I could not turn to face her.

When the sun rose to wake me from my staring, I dragged up my stiffened back bone and visited the carpenter and the blacksmith. I requested they build her a coffin with the mattress stuffing, glass, and wood. Three days later, I lay her in the coffin and lightly clasp the door closed. I placed my wrists against it, fearing to smudge the perfect glass with tear-stained, soiled fingertips. I would not bury her here. I would take her back to her clearing, by the rubble of stone where I first met her. She had not visited her village since that time. Her spirit could wander her forest and relive the childhood

Eulogy

memories until I avenged her death.

Voices streamed from outside the window that woke me from my melancholy.

"It's a miracle!"

"Did you hear? Did you hear?"

"The Galilean, Jesus, it's a miracle!"

I stepped outside to listen to the rambling closer.

"What's going on?" I wiped the tears form my eyes as I nudged a bystander.

"Jesus of Nazareth has raised Lazarus from the dead!"

"Where is he?" I asked.

"I don't know. I heard this from travelers in the East. The miracle happened in Bethany"

Confusion and anger flooded my psyche. I rushed to Pontius Pilate with the news. I explained to him about Oriana.

"That is regrettable about your wife. I will grant you three days furlough for your loss."

"Thank you, sir. The Galilean was in Bethany."

If I ever got my hands on that man, I would ask him why he was where my Oriana was not. Who was this *Lazarus* to him that he would spare his life and not my Oriana's? The loss of Oriana was unbearable and I knew my revenge would vindicate it. This *Galilean* whose tradition had allowed such laws to exist in his very own time: he would dare to save one of his own but not a Samaritan? This is all I knew of him. He had the power, from where ever that power may come from, but he failed to use it when it was inconvenient for him.

I wrote to Leander in Mesopotamia of the tragedy and asked that he would request furlough to be stationed here with me. I promised I would take care of his expenses. I still had the slip to go to the bank, though the thought of going to the bank without Oriana pained me terribly. The salary meant nothing without her.

Traveling to the clothes shop, I found a long brown robe and clothed it over my red tunic. I went to the marketplace clearing, pulled up a chair, listening. Any travelers that would speak about the incident, I followed and interrogated. I might have been new to Jerusalem, but fear tactics worked the same all over the known world. I had connections of my own. I would find the murderers, and take my vengeance. I would inevitably confront the one that neglected her life.

Eulogy

Escalating back to my lonely home, I found the names of the murderers, men and women alike after one day's work. I looked up their addresses at the census directory and mulled on how I would take their lives. I lit incense in the room around her and lit her favorite candles. I set Diana statues on top of her coffin to watch over her as she wondered in the afterlife. Lifting the glass, I put two coins on her lids to pay Chiron. My death would be much different. If, dying in battle, as a soldier passes, they are burned. Looking at her perfect fawn like features, her autumn colored hair, and flower lips, I could not bear the thought of turning it to ashes or putting it in the ground, not now at least. Anger made me strong for her. Choking back the tears again, I let her sleep on the Egyptian mattress forever. After my vengeance was accomplished, I would be of no more service to Pilate. I would ask to be stationed back at Rome. Oriana would come with me then and she would be at peace when I was in mine.

"My strength is dried up like a potsherd, and my tongue sticks to the roof of my mouth, you lay me in the dust of death. Dogs have surrounded me; a band of evil men has encircled me, they have pierced my hands and my feet. I can count all my bones; people stare and gloat over me. They divide my garments amongst them and cast lots for my clothes." - Psalm 22:15-18

Vengeance

"This man is a menace to our whole way of life. We must be rid of him," a short barrel figured man groaned as he stood before the Sanhedrin in the House of Caiaphas. "How can someone say they will tear down the holy temple and rebuild it in three days?!"

"Here, here, I agree, he told us this as we confronted him on what he said about us being like sepulchers: white on the outside but, full of death within," another one appalled. "This man knows nothing of who we are; just who does *he* think *he is?*"

"Well, he is no worse that John the Baptist. You know what happened to him." Caiaphas smugly mentioned.

"The people see him as a god and a king. He performs magic and promotes heresy," another pointed out.

"Then, since he is in this part of the known

world more than at other times of travel, it will not be long: we will trap him."

"I know some of them that follow him. We could seek audience with one of them."

"Do you think he will betray his *master?*" Caiaphas questioned in shock.

"We will make it worth his while. Thirty silver coins should be a good price that is less than half a ransom for a king. We do not want the man to know we think he is that much of a threat. I had a dream that he would come to us. This must be a sign."

The barrel shaped man nodded, "What is his name?"

"Judas of Iscariot."

I knew Bethany was not very far away. One of the men spoke of him in Rome. The woman wanted to travel to Jerusalem to use his powers for her son. My vengeance would shortly be fulfilled.

I quietly stalked the murderers: sitting at the

Eulogy

marketplace, listening for their name to be used. Then, as night fell, they receded to their rat holes. I waited for them to fall asleep. All of them, throat slit, as they slept: dreaming sweet dreams. This was a better death then Oriana suffered, but this Galilean would be harder to find, so I had to be a ghost as he was. My three day furlough ended and I reported to the praetorium.

"I will need you to stay over tonight. We are expecting a visitor. The Sanhedrin believes that they may have trapped the Galilean and it is good that you have reported on this day. He will be in your charge, if he is found guilty. For his crimes, the Sanhedrin will see that he is crucified by Roman law. They see him as a heretic, magician, and an enemy against the empire. The people see him as a king and a god. It is in my right and power as Governor to judge him for these crimes accordingly. They know where he is going to be and they will be judging them their selves tonight."

My mind swam with thoughts of glee. I fought a smile leaping at my expression. He would be judged. I would be able to find him and he would be right here in front of me. It would be so hard to control myself with him only a few feet away from me. I gritted my teeth in the thought.

"Because, you will be here over night, I will give you leave to rest if you wish or you may stay in my quarters while I work and I will call for a replacement. I have come to like you in the short time I have known you, soldier. You are very obedient and ask little of me. Would this accommodate or be a silent request of yours. Why do you glare so?"

I calmed my expression at these words of suspicion.

"Oh, no, your honor, I glare so, because I mourn still. I cannot go home. I did not have the heart to put her in the ground."

Pilate looked solemnly at the floor, "I understand. Again, I express greatest solemn for your loss, son. The offer still stands."

"I cannot sleep," I replied.

"Some lunch?"

"No, your honor, I have all the fuel I need."

He ascended, "Well, then...I put your wine skin

Eulogy

in the kitchen, and if you ever change your mind, you are welcome to my accommodations."

"Thank you, sir."

"Guard the gate until you are called. Another guard is out there if you need to rest."

"Thank you, sir."

His kindness was welcomed in my state, but irritating. It reminded me of the state I was in. This was the worst thing: standing here, listening to the same old gossip. How was I supposed to fuel my anger, stay on fire, amp myself for the confrontation? Patience was no longer my prize virtue: waiting and watching the sun. The soldier beside me tried to make casual conversation. I spoke not. I looked not at him. I glared only for the shadow of the sun on the buildings in front of me. If only something would happen. I wished for anarchy. I imagined some bystanders would start a riot. I wanted an excuse to kill.

Then my thoughts turned to realize that the gods were trying to teach me temperance. My time *would come.* I needed to be calm. Pontius Pilate would surely find him guilty and I would be there. I would see him die. If not by my own hand, I would revel in it. If given this power he was expected to act.

I could feel my eyes burning. My Oriana, how I missed her glistening hair, the feel of her warmth beside me as we slept. Her beautiful teeth smiling at me with the surprises she would "buy for me." A tear fell on my tunic. I quickly wiped it away and the anger seethed. I was nothing without her: a hollow empty space, a torn bleeding heart. Anger replaced all my love for her. It was my only fire now.

After the goal was attained, I would have no more to live for. I would jump to the Sirens by the Pillars of Hercules. Their song would guide me to whatever afterlife there is for me now. Leander would come and find the abandoned home. I would cash in my two hundred and fifty thousand dollars slip; leave it with the rest of the cash, and a note welcoming him to my life.

Hades was the only destination for me now. I would plead my case to Chiron to let me see Oriana one last time before the torturous hands ripped my

Eulogy

soul apart, over and over until the earth was destroyed. Or perhaps, my forever would be to be the food for Cerberus. That forever wouldn't be so bad if he started from head to toe, until the next day. At least it would be sporadic, nothing the same every time the sun set on earth: or better . . . an eternity of fighting the Hydra. That would be exciting! Every battle would end with a different winner.

"Quittin' Time," the soldier glanced at me, dousing my fire to reality. The shadows had reached well below the rooftops. The sun's sliver grazed the hillside. I retreated into Pilate's residence.

I stood beside where Pontius would sit at his desk, waiting. My mind was blank. I only felt anticipation. For hours I stood...waiting. The soldier that guarded the entrance of the residence walked towards me, awakening me from my stare, beat his chest and bowed.

"The Sanhedrin is here and requests the Governor step outside. Their religion prohibits them from entering. It is their Passover."

A.R. Perkins

"I will summon him from slumber," I replied.

I ascended the stair well to the main residence and spoke with the soldier standing guard at his chamber door. I whispered the message in his ear. He nodded and went inside to rouse him.

I descended back to my station and waited for orders.

"He will be down shortly," I told the guard.

He stood on the other side of the grand dark wood desk and waited. The Governor descended motioned to both of us to follow him. We arrived in front of Sanhedrin, two holding the arms of a tall bearded man in white clothing.

"What charges are you bringing against this man?"

"If he were not a criminal, we would not have handed him over to you. We have no right to execute anyone."

Pilate went back inside and the two of us grabbed the accused and followed him. We released our grip and we stood on either side as we were originally. This was *it*. I had no way to kill this neglectful man now. My thoughts tried not to

Eulogy

recede to my love as she lay encased in eternal beauty. I had to remain calm and await his judgment. Imprisonment would only keep me from my intentions for Leander and to bury Oriana. The man looked at me for only a moment, his eyes stern but sensitive, as though he could read my thoughts.

"Are you the king of the Jews," Pilate asked.

"Is that idea of your own accord or did others tell you this?"

Pilate retorted, "Am I a Jew? It was your own people that accuse you and hand you to me. What is it you have done to be so accused?"

The man explained, "My kingdom is not of this world."

"You are a king, then?"

"Yes, it is as you say. I was born to testify to the truth, but my kingdom is from another place. If I were a king of this world, my servants would fight to prevent this arrest."

"What other charges do they bring against you?"

The man said nothing. Pilate waited but his patience for the answer only astounded him.

A.R. Perkins

Pilate's wife stood at the top threshold and waved to him. He ascended to her and she whispered something to him. I could not make it out. He nudged her elbow lightly and waved her back to bed, and then he returned to his seat.

"What *is* truth?" He only muttered this to himself, and then spoke aloud, "I find no fault in this man."

My vengeance would have to be found by other mean. This could not be it. I gritted my teeth in anger. It was now morning, and many people had gather in the square. The Sanhedrin waited outside to hear of the man's fate. My eyes grazed over the size of the crowd. The Galilean was a very well-known man.

Behind the Sanhedrin, stood a tall pale man, his head rose from under his black hood and as my eyes found him in the crowd. His eyes glared at me. They looked like stones, completely black; the whites of his eyes were not visible. His hands were folded. I stared a bit at him and his eyes got harder. It was hard to force my gaze away. As Pilate spoke, I turned to his voice.

Eulogy

"I find no guilt in this man, but it is customary for your Passover for me to release one prisoner. Do you want me to release this 'King of the Jews'?'"

The crowded shouted emphatically, "No! Crucify him! Crucify him!"

"Give us Barabbas," another shouted. He was no doubt one of the conspirators in the rebellion. Barabbas killed many during the onslaught.

The man in the black robe reiterated, "Give us Barabbas!" The crowd repeated.

"And what should I do with *this* man" Pilate asked to confirm.

"Crucify him," the man in black answered.

"Yes, CRUCIFY HIM!!!" the crowd repeated again and again they chanted.

"Bring me my water pitcher and basin and set it in front of me" Pilate ordered his quarter-guard. He retrieved the items and Pilate motioned him as he held his hands over the basin. The soldier poured the water on his hands.

He shouted to the crowd over their chants, "Let this be a symbol that this man's blood is not on my hands, but on the hands of the Jews."

The crowd chanted simultaneously and monotone,

"Let it be on our hands and on the hands of our children."

They seemed possessed. What had these kinfolk of theirs done to deserve such hate? He healed *their* people, but not my love. *I* had a reason to hate him for his inaction. This made me all the angrier. Was there some predetermined cause for his fate? What power did this man in black have over them that they repeated everything he proposed? My suspicion was unanswered and I remained curious. All the while the crowd deafened me with their shouts. I strained to hear what Pilate had to say.

"Remember, soldier, he is in your charge. The Jews have found him guilty though he is still under Roman rule. Even though we are not responsible for his death, from now until Sunday night you must guard him, dead or alive. His followers are too afraid to save him and have fled, but they still believe that he is their Messiah. We fear they will

Eulogy

try to stage a resurrection by robbing his grave. You will delegate the punishment, Centurion, and guard his burial personally."

"Thank you, your honor; I will not let you down."

"Good, we do not need another uprising or rebellion."

The Centurion of this legion was inconveniently murdered by Barabbas. I would be replacing him on the short notice of this problematic situation. Pilate got up and walked to his armory. He handed me the cat of nine tails.

"I do not want to crucify the man. My wife told me of a dream she had last night. She told me not to judge this man in ill favor. She said that Rome would burn and all Roman leaders would be killed. Let him be flogged and mortified. Perhaps that would appease the Jews. Since they see him as their king, let us mock him in that manner. Surely, their hearts will soften and open their eyes to the brutality. I fear an uprising will occur if something is not done."

"Yes your honor, I will do as you say."

A.R. Perkins

Still no appeasement for me though. My heart still harbored the pain. I summoned the soldiers at the Fish Gate and the Sheep Gate and replaced them with other guards not on duty that lived nearby. These two gates were not in great need of guarding, so the time it took for them to report would not be missed. This commotion had the entire city out of their beds and followed me and the Galilean near the Antonia Fortress. I explained the situation to the guards, and one handed me a creative crown of thorns he had collected vines from and intertwined.

"Good thinking, soldier. We will pound it on his head with a staff after he is flogged," I said.

"You may address me as Stephaton, sir."

He smiled at me, trying to gain approval of him in my new position.

I stood in front of the accused, and glared up at him with all the anger I had in me. His eyes touched mine for only a moment and then stared in front of him. I punched him square in the jaw a head taller than my own, trying to incite. No different was his reaction.

Trying to rip his tunic apart with no avail, I

Eulogy

pulled the tunic over his head. I noticed the threads were sown horizontally so no sword would do better than my own two hands. This was all the more frustrating. I pushed him to the stone pavement, dragged him back up, and tied his hands around the whipping post at the wrists. I tied his feet at the ankles to the small protrusion of stone at the other end. His back left no indentation. I wanted this to hurt. I wanted him to feel the pain that my Oriana knew before she died. Maybe then, he would know his miraculous powers were all for nothing.

I drew back the cat of nine tails and wretched my arm forward on his bare flesh. He did not cry out. Again, I lashed forward . . . nothing. Forty times, I tore the flesh from him. No response. I heard him seethe through his teeth, the last ten lashes, but no cry of pain. I untied him and Stephaton and I roughly jerked him up. The proving soldier put a purple and red velour robe on the man's back. Then, we beat the crown of thorns he had made on the man's head with a staff. The thorns were four inches long and pierced far into his skull. If the cross didn't kill him, the loss of blood would. Still, I was not satisfied.

My Oriana suffered, but she did not live. Her crime was nothing. She was different, that's all. Her innocent light was infectious and there was no cause for her to feel anything that she did not deserve in return. We took him back to Pilate at the praetorium headquarters and displayed him before Pilate. He looked at him and shuddered. He then stood, raised his palm in the accused direction to address the crowd.

"Here is the man." The shouting had all died down, until we returned. Then the vibrating chants began again. The marble stone sang their echoes. They were out for blood not the gore of his suffering.

The persona of curiosity glared at me coldly and smiled. His chest and shoulders vibrated as if he were laughing, but I could not hear. He remained to see this murder through, the one he had caused.

"*You* take him and crucify him. I find no guilt *in this man!*" Pilate's voice cracked and he uncharacteristically rose up along with his hands towards the Galilean."

Eulogy

The Jewish leaders retorted, "*Our* law says that he must be killed, because he claims to be the son of God."

Pilate returned to his desk and summoned the Galilean.

"Answer me this," he ordered the accused, "where do you come from?"

No replied was uttered.

"You realize that your brethren gave you to me to pronounce judgment upon you? I hold your fate in my hands. I have the power to have you *crucified*?" Pilate was louder than ever at these questions, pleading this man would speak and give testimony to his innocence.

Finally, the accused explained, "You would have no power over me if you were not given it by My Father. The one who handed me to you is guilty of a greater sin."

Pilate again looked at the crowd. He attempted one last time to reason with the borderline rioters.

"My laws and beliefs are not your laws and beliefs. You here live under Roman law and I am here to keep the peace," Pilate explained. "Am I so

A.R. Perkins

much different from this man? I am not monotheistic. I care not about your laws. I uphold the laws of Caesar; therefore, I cannot *find* any law that exists in the Twelve Tables or find it in my soul to condemn this man to death. Do you not see that he has been punished enough?"

The crowd saw this as a weakness and went for his metaphoric jugular. "If you let this man free, you are no friend to Caesar. Anyone who says they are a king opposes Caesar."

Pilate was only angered at this, since they did *have a king* only a stone's throw from the temple. He angrily sauntered to the praetorium door motioning us to follow him with the man. He parted the crowd. The people spat on the accused as we passed. We walked towards the temple.

Pilate took him by the arm and led him to the Gabbatha. Those who passed judgment sat on this stone elevation. My partner in this act knelt down with the staff we used to put the crown on the accused head, and laid the mockery on thick, "Hail king of the Jews!"

Pilate began a tirade to the accusers, "If he is

Eulogy

not a king of this world, then logic tells me he should not be seated at Herod's palace. So let his judgment be put upon you in *his* kingdom. You yourself stated you wanted him dead because he claims to be the son of your God. Am I so different, that I do not believe in your ways? If he is the son of your God and he came to this world to testify the truth, then let him judge you before your God. I will not crucify him. Here is your King!"

The man in black laughed darkly. The Sanhedrin cringed. The crowd groaned.

"TAKE HIM AWAY! CRUCIFY HIM! CRUCIFY HIM!"

Pilate was emphatic with a hint of confused sarcasm, *"Shall I crucify your king?"*

The man in black shouted, "We have no king but Caesar," The Sanhedrin repeated.

The crowded repeated then with raised enthusiasm.

The accused looked at Pilate, returning his sorrowful and regretful gaze, "You would have no power over me if it were not given. My kingdom is not of this world."

A.R. Perkins

Pilate collapsed onto the elevated place holding his head in his hands. I could see his face cringed in pain and he swallowed hard. He looked up at me, his eyes red, and waved a gesture at me.

"Take him away."

I saw Pilate retreated to the praetorium, his cape waving behind him: portraying his angry expression. I motioned to Stephaton. I noticed the accused wince as I stripped the robe off his back, opening the old wounds as the blood started to dry. I motioned to him as I clothed him as a young child with his old white garments. Why he could not do this himself, I wondered. I was his charge but not his mother.

We took him to the armory in the Essence Quarter and lugged the largest cross to match his stature. The weight was taxing him to where he was down to my height. Wielding the staff, I nudged him on. We would guard him from there to Golgotha outside the second quarter wall. His weariness must have blinded him. He tripped over a loose stone and the cross plunged him to the ground.

Eulogy

Before I could bark at him to get up and beat him with the staff, a woman came out of the crowd and wiped his face with her veil. He thanked her by grabbing her wrist ever so gently then, trudged up his shoulders and went on. My anger descended slightly at the sight of this. I was in awe of the obedience of his fate, but I could not back out now. My thoughts remembered my debt to Pilate and to Oriana.

The anger soon flooded over me again. I growled at him to keep moving and hurry his pace. He only half obeyed and I struck him with the staff in my anger. I wanted him to fall at my blow but he disappointed me. I wanted an excuse to kill him then, but I had to obey as well. He was ordered to be crucified, and we still had a long way to go. The patience at Pilate's residence came to me again, temporarily.

Many women came to him after the bravery of the other. They were crying softly. I looked at them and my heart was touched. Stephaton allowed them to pass as well.

The man looked at them and paused, "Weep not

for me. Weep for your selves and for you children. The day will come when barren wombs will be revered. People will say 'mountains, fall on us!' and 'hills, cover us!' for if this happens when the grass are green, what will happen when it is dry?

He fell again, and I lifted him up.

"Surely he will die before he makes it," Stephaton noticed in fear. I looked around and found a great muscular man.

"You, sir, *come here*! Help this man."

I cared not who he was. We were almost to the place of skull. Issachar, Gad, Matthias, Barnabas, and Simon were there. Gad held a sign made by Pilate in three languages that said, 'Jesus of Nazareth: King of the Jews.' So, *that* was his name. My anger blinded me to his identity. How different was he really from my Oriana? The people wanted him dead for their laws. Why did the crowd follow the man in black so? He remained, watching. I did not have time for regret or confusion. I wiped my mind clean of these questions. The path had been laid out for me. I had to follow it through. My anger returned, but it had

Eulogy

no more fuel or reason. It was now a habit I could not break.

Stephaton, both Simons, and I lugged the cross up the hill to the crucifixion site. Issachar, Gad and Matthias led Jesus up the hill. The three laid him on the cross. Matthias on the left, Gad on the right, spread his arms as far as they would go. Simultaneous, they took the ten inch spikes and placed them over his wrists after marking the separation in the bones. Issachar overlapped his feet on the cross' protrusion and started to pound the spike into them. Jesus cried out, "Father, forgive them, for they do not know what they are doing!"

All of us lifted the cross into the hole that they dug out and drove wedges in to secure it. His body jarred at the abruptness of the fall. If not for the ropes fastening him at they forearms, he would have been ripped apart.

I noticed the sky began to darken. It looked as though the sun, though high in the sky, was setting. I looked up and saw the sun began to wane behind a dark orb.

The High Priest of the Pharisees shouted to

the onlookers, "He claims to be the son of God. Let us see him come down then. Let God rescue him now."

The accused on the left said, "Yes, save yourself. Save us."

The accused on the right said, "Have you no fear of the world to come? We deserve our fate, this man does not. Jesus, remember me when you come into your kingdom."

Jesus said to him, "Surely, this day you will be with me in paradise."

A sad look came on the face of Jesus. The clouds came in and the darkness deepened. The darkness seemed to cloud his soul.

"My God, My God, why have you forsaken me?" Stephaton made a sponge on a hyssop branch soaked in wine vinegar. The Pharisee said, "Leave him be He calls to Elijah. Let Him save him now."

The hate and insensitivity unnerved me. Was I so different only hours ago? I seemed to be looking in a mirror as I gazed sharply at the Pharisee. Stephaton was my soldier. What right did he have to order him so?

Eulogy

Jesus breathed his last breath. A terrible earthquake shook and opened the earth in front of the hill. The man in black fell into the hole along with a few others that could not get out of the way fast enough.

My mind was astounded at this, I spoke my thoughts aloud, "Truly, this man was the Son of God."

The other soldiers looked at me in disbelief, and then genuflected at Jesus' body. We did not break his legs, for we thought he was already dead. The deed had to be done completely. All my anger and hate turned to confusion. My only recourse to be cleansed was to perform one final act: my own final act. I put all my sorrow, all my hate, all my anger, all my joyful memories of Oriana into this final act. I took my spear and drove it into Jesus' side with force. Blood and water exploded out of the wound and sprayed my face. I breathed it and my gritted teeth were covered in it.

"Rag!" I ordered one. One gave me the tunic he won in the gambling activity. I wiped my face. The ingestion could not be helped, but I swigged my mouth with my wine skin. The blood was sweet. It did not taste like I thought it would. Almost like honey and fruit. The smell stayed in my nose. It reminded me of roses and honeysuckle vine.

Now I was thoroughly confused. I started to panic. My heart started thumping furiously, and then stopped all together. Had I just died? My eyes were opened. My limbs moved. My brain worked. No, I was not asleep, or was I? What was wrong with me?

A man came to me and interrupted my rambling thoughts.

"I would like to have the body and prepare it before the Sabbath begins."

I looked at him, and nodded, "Just lead me to where it will be. I must stand guard."

He nodded. We walked around the wall past the Fish Gate to the tomb. I still had the spear in hand. After the woman at the crucifixion site had prepared the body, the man placed Jesus into the tomb. I rolled the large stone into the front, which seemed easier than it should have been to do.

The next day, a dark oily haired soldier named

Eulogy

Petronius reported to me. His frame was gangly but he was shorter than I. "The Sanhedrin wanted the tomb as secure as possible, so they went to Pilate and requested another guard be posted, just in case you slept." His green eyes were striking as he gazed at me when he spoke.

I looked down and answered, "I have not slept and will not. My charged order was until Sunday night. Do they not know the penalty for sleeping on duty is death?"

Petronius shrugged his shoulders. "They only know the laws that most benefit them. Besides, even a centurion should be held accountable."

I growled in discontent.

"Being that *I am* the Centurion of this region now, I will say who guards what, not them. But since it was an order from Pilate, I will grant *great* leniency to you. You may do as you wish and I will pledge you were here the whole time, you may sleep, eat, stand on your head, whatever."

"I have nothing better to do. Might as well get paid justly for my work right? But I will take you up on the sleeping part."

A.R. Perkins

"So, who was this guy we are guarding," Petronius asked.

"Rumors say he performed miracles and many believe that he was the son of their god. After being at his crucifixion, I can tell you that the rumors are true. I do not believe as they believe, and never have, but the sun turned black and the earth broke apart. Surely *something* unworldly was angry at his son's death.

"All I know is that I am stronger now than I have ever been. I do not have the urge to sleep and I have been up for five straight days. I just lost my wife to the corrupt laws these people follow. He was also a victim of such laws. The world is not the same as it was when these laws were written. How could they still adhere to them?"

"I don't know, sir. I am sorry to hear of your loss."

I glared at him, "I did not mention my loss for your sorrow soldier. I mentioned it only to prove a point. This spear or I have brought this difference on. My heart no longer beats in my chest, but here I sit beside you, having a conversation."

Eulogy

Petronius stood up, fear on his face. "What are you then if not alive?"

"I do not know. All I know is that I thirst."

"These people come near to me with their mouth and honor me with their lips, but their hearts are far from me. Their worship of me is made up of only rules taught by men."   - Isaiah 29:13

Esoteric

Petronius started to run away. Like lightening I flashed at him and grabbed him. My fingers dented purple marks on the blood that pulsed from his arm. His throat pulsed as well. We zapped behind the tomb as I bit into the pulsing veins. The honey and fruit taste came back again, and I could not stop. Every part of me said to go on, except for the heart I once had.

The sorrow came back again before I bled him dry.

"What am I doing?"

This man had done nothing to me. I stopped; my thoughts woke me from my frenzy. The grey limp guard looked at me in fear. I got up from him and started to think panicking. I must make this right. How could my soul ever find its way for *even one* small glimpse of Oriana like this?

If this man in the tomb was the son of a god, his blood must be the cause for my change. Now I was a monster. My anger and hatred in my action against him bled through to this 'after life.' Could I even die now that I was already dead?

A.R. Perkins

I would make this sin against Petronius right. I could be purged, I hoped. Petronius was at the verge of death, he would die. The only life I could give him would be one like my own. I rolled the stone away from the tomb. I took a chalice from my bag. I found it by the high priest's house in the Essence Quarter. I thought it a neat little thing, lying at the stair well, while the accused was given his cross. Oriana would have liked it.

I rolled back the stone with ease. I moved the linen he was wrapped in and found the scar I had left. I took the chalice under it, close to his skin, and pushed on his chest. Nothing came out. I must have killed him then, he was definitely dead now and the blood had coagulated. My thoughts flew sporadically. My victim would die before my ignorance could be abolished. Think. . .

I rolled the stone back. What should I do? I tried to pierce my own skin with my teeth. The sound sent shivers down my spine. I feared my teeth were cracked. Looking at my wrist, tiny scars remained and did not heal. I felt my teeth with thumb and finger tips, but they were unscathed. Think . . .

Eulogy

I took my sword and cringed for the same metallic sound. It did not disappoint. My wrist remained whole with only the teeth marks I had left. Shavings of metal lay on the ground.

Think . . .

The only other weapon I had on me at that time was the spear. I pierced the point stained with the blood of the accused into the meatiest part of my palm. If I had ingested his blood, then my blood must be as his own. I drained it into the chalice. Blood slowly started to release but stopped when the spear was removed. The wound closed over instantly.

I rushed to Petronius, his eyes closed now. Was I too late? I opened his mouth and fed him the contents. I had done all I could do and waited back at front of the tomb. Hearing a rustle in the night's silence, I returned to Petronius. He was sitting in the brush of the trees.

"What did you do to me?" He looked at me in fright and disgust.

"I gave you life, friend."

"You are no friend to me."

"I told you my story. I don't understand it

either. Now you are like me."

"What will my family say when they see me like this? I do not want to maul them as you have done to me?"

"My remorse is too great to bear on my discretion towards you Petronius. The only answer I can give to you on that quandary is that you may not want to see them again."

"I *hate you* for this, Centurion. You made me a servant of death."

I did feel great sorrow for what I had done to him. The only resolution I could give him was to become invisible now to the life he once had. I had no ties now, none to speak of. I had left my own family long ago, tenderly at fourteen. Oriana and I took care of each other in those days, when we were slaves to the servitude of Rome. Her charge to me was her only safety, my charge to her my only reason for living.

His hateful words targeted as vapor. I became acceptant of this after life quickly, but I still longed for death. I supposed I got my wish. I was truly, as Petronius as so wisely said, a servant of death. We had no purpose, no fuel, no need, no love, no life,

Eulogy

and no laughter inside.

Soon after, the sun was rising and hung low in the sky. Only a day to go and I would cash in the slip and bury Oriana. Two of the women from the crucifixion came to check on the tomb. We stared at them and wondered why they were there. The earth shook and a white robed man that shown like the sun grazing on snow tops rolled the stone back, laid it on the ground with ease, and sat on it. We were frozen in fear.

The bright man looked at the woman and said, "Do not be afraid. Jesus is not here. He is risen and alive. Go see, and then tell His followers. He is going to Galilee and you will see Him there."

They ran away saying praises.

The bright man looked at us.

"You two on the other hand, Jesus has a very different mission for you."

"What has happened to me?" I asked.

"This man mauled my throat and nearly killed me. What mission could you possibly have for me?" Petronius was very confused.

"My name is Gabriel. I am the servant of the one and almighty God. There are no others, only

Him. The fables you were told in your youth were tales man made to explain their emptiness and things created. You are now servants as well but not like me."

I looked at him in great disgust saying bitterly, "I am *no* servant of any *god*. I serve myself. My wife was killed by the very laws *your god* made."

He then reached at me quicker than light, grabbed my tunic, and glared at me. I looked into his omniscient eyes defiantly and saw Oriana on fire. I grabbed Gabriel by his cloak at the chest and gripped in anger and pain, screaming tears that would not come.

"This was the fate of all who believe your ways. The only way to find peace is to believe in the sacrifice the Son of God made. All men and woman are sinful. Her *precious Diana* did not save her, nor did she save her child."

He said this with great sarcasm. I glared at him in anger and grit my teeth.

He continued, ignoring me, "The only way for you to be what you are was to present you with a reason to hate. Now your hate and anger have cursed you to wander the earth until the end of it.

Eulogy

You will not find peace until you take the spear and kill Satan in the form of man. The same spear that killed Christ is the only thing that will kill his counterpart."

"How am I supposed to do this? You entrapped me into your service, just what if *I kill you now*?" I seethed again.

"Would that be wise? You are only one man, now two. Heaven is filled with ones such as me: as many as the stars.

"Would you serve him, Petronius?"

"Only if it meant I could die," he answered.

"This is the way of it then. You are soulless men. Lucifer can only see the souls of men. I, too, am hidden from his site, for I have no soul. I am a created servant, a messenger, an Archangel, one of the highest seraphim in the King's court. I tell you this because; the one who created you planned your actions the day you were born, as he did you Petronius, as he did Judas Iscariot."

"So where are our souls?" Petronius asked.

"Have you ever heard of the mythological beast, whose identity could only been seen by the pure of heart?"

We looked at each other and nodded.

"You will notice that your Rosalba is gone. The day Jesus returns, he will ride her in the sky. Your souls and all those you create will be encased in her horn. The more souls, the larger it will become. When she can no longer raise her head, the time will come. No one will see her until such time, not here or in Heaven. Only the Lord will know."

"So why do you really need us? You have not explained our mission. Yes, I understand that the 'Anti-Christ' must be slain, but does he not have powers of his own?"

Gabriel chuckled, "I thought a Centurion like you would've figured this out by now. You must create an army. You have been chosen for your loyalty and love of human life. You can seek out the souls that need saving and the men will follow your every word.

"The spear cannot be taken. It has powers of its own, besides the obvious extinction of the unclean one."

"But if I create ones like me, will they not thirst as I do? I cannot sleep, or eat."

"Hence, the beauty of it, you will never tire.

Eulogy

There are many missions in your life's work that are planned for you. Before the Anti-Christ comes, you will guard the scrolls that will become our holy book. You will guard the mother of Jesus until her time has ended on this earth. You will keep on you the holy chalice you found safe from the evil doers. You will do many things. I will ever be in your mind when the time is needed for you. I will come if ever you need me. I will ever mold your steps to where you are needed. Now go to your home, Leander waits for you there. Take Oriana to Rome and lay her to rest."

Gabriel disappeared. Petronius followed me to my abode. I would be loyal to this Jesus. It was the only thing I could do. I deserved to be blackmailed, but there were many things that I was not aware of before. Why did I not take a different action when I heard the rumors, Follow Jesus where he led, and take Oriana with me? Reject all fictitious beliefs. My eyes were opened now, though it was a bit late. I would find myself in Heaven...someday.

Gabriel had awakened me to another fact of who the man in black was. He assisted in the murder of Jesus. I had the same powers, yielding the spear and partaking in the Son of Man, which he had. I could make others follow my instruction and never hurt an innocent soul. Gabriel would pick out every man I would ever need in this army of God. We stopped by my abode.

"Petronius, go tell Pilate what happened. Leave out the part about Gabriel and his words to us, though. We cannot tell another soul, his mind would be tainted and Lucifer will know of the plans."

"Yes, my leader."

I entered and Leander had let himself in, "How did you make it so fast, my friend? You left only a week ago."

"I never left. I came by to see how things were."

I answered him by opening the bedroom door. Seeing the coffin, Leander dropped his grand frame to his knees in sorrow.

"I wrote you a letter, but I suppose you did not receive it."

CVIII

Eulogy

He shook his head, still bowing. As my explanation progressed, his fists tightened.

"I am going to take her to Rome. Will you come with me?"

"Yes, my friend."

"I have to do something first. I had plans for you, Leander. I was going to jump off the cliff at the Pillars of Hercules and leave you with this home. Now, it seems I will need the money. The man they crucified was the Son of the only Almighty God."

"What are you talking about," Leander asked.

"Would you serve me no matter what, Leander?"

"Yes," he said.

"I want you to do something for me. You will be my second in command."

"Anything for you, my friend," he promised.

"Even if it meant you would die?"

"Yes, I would follow you anywhere, till the end."

I took the chalice out of my bag again and went over the same scar with my spear. Leader looked at me inquisitively.

CIX

A.R. Perkins

"Drink this, Leander, and fulfill this vow. I will tell you everything."

"Will it kill me?"

"Yes, but I am already dead."

Leander looked more than confused and also a bit concerned now. Perhaps it was for my sanity. He must have thought I meant it metaphorically. I needed him though, someone not a puppet to Gabriel's powers. He drank it. I heard his heart pounding rapidly...then it stopped. I explained the mission we were to undertake.

He looked at me and said, "I always wanted to live forever. This was the *greatest thing* you could've given me, friend. I didn't feel a thing."

"It is a gift from God, Leander, but you are cursed until Lucifer is slain by *this* spear."

"Cursed? You must be joking. How could *this* be a curse?"

He laughed robust echoes throughout the marble home. Petronius came inside. He could see Leander was just like us.

"Just how many army members does this Gabriel need? We are changelings . . . no more than mythical half breeds of life and death. This whole

Eulogy

thing is completely disgusting, and you are going to give in to that blackmailer's commands?"

"Petronius, would you like to see your family again?"

He nodded solemnly.

"I, too, have loved ones I wish to see, namely her," I motioned to the coffin. Petronius' face softened, all anger and confusion had gone away from his features. He looked at Oriana and smiled.

"We must get going on our journey. I do not know how much time we have."

That information was completely vacant from the revealing conversation.

We left to the stable and sure enough Rosalba was gone. Marcellus and Brutus were inside. We went to the stable and looked for a horse for Petronius. The fur was pale colored with a hint of green in the shadow of it. This horse was different and it caught my eye as though I was drawn to it. Brutus' color had changed slightly as well. I noticed the shades of brown turn scarlet in places.

We traveled to the lamnia. I cashed in the slip. I made travel arrangements with the same sailor Peregrine to leave as soon as possible. We rode back to our home and loaded Oriana into the wagon. This would be our home when we returned. The scrolls would be written soon and I would have to delegate who to guard them. As we boarded the boat, Peregrine eyed our horses oddly, and then went up to the helm.

We sat in the cargo hold and discussed our plans. Leander looked pensive, so I asked him what he was thinking about.

"I was thinking I should change my name. I have a new life now, so why not a new name."

"I, too, need to change my name," I said. My name means 'vain.' That would be no name for a Centurion of God. This spear will be my inspiration."

"Petronius means 'guarding shield.' I feel a consuming morbidity in this new life. My horse looks like sickness."

We laughed, it was true. The green came out more and more as the days went on.

Leander seemed ferocious as he clenched his fist, stating "I will be the catalyst of this war at the end. They may start the fight, but I will help you end it swiftly. These new teeth of mine will rip the

Eulogy

demons to shreds. You can be the Centurion, but I will be the Second-in-Command, your Lieutenant, in a sense. I am Ardin Pyralis: 'the fiery one of fire.' Brutus will ignite under my groins as the war rages on." His eyes gleamed at this thought."

"You can have it," the newly named Thanos said. "My horse will be called 'Fatality Rampageous.'"

"Marcellus seems as good of a name as any for my horse. I will keep it for the memory of my Oriana." We all looked at her, only a few feet from us, as I said it.

"GABRIEL!" I shouted.

He appeared before us, in a flash of lightening, as he had promised he would if I need him.

"Yes?" He answered irritated. "You know I have other things to attend to. I am bonded to your will as you are to mine."

"Can you not let her be extinguished until my mission is complete? Is there not a *better* place in Hades you can put her until then? I will be comforted in the fact that she will burn if I do not fulfill my word."

"That is not in my hands," he explained.

A.R. Perkins

"*LOOK AT HER!*" I screamed in disgust.

"I feel not the emotions you do. I move the pieces in the game. She is a pawn."

I growled at him.

"Can you not do *anything*? Let me speak with Jesus then. Surely He would know how I feel. He will answer me. His miracles so powerful here on earth, can He not do *something*?"

"Pray," Gabriel said.

"He is elsewhere in Galilee is He not?" I was confused at how he could hear me there.

Gabriel paused and again said, "Pray."

I took Gabriel's cloak to hold him fast to me as I wrenched it and spoke quietly to myself.

"Be still, my soldier." His voice said inside me. "Behold Gabriel's eyes."

I got up and looked into Gabriel's eyes. Oriana sat in darkness, by a fiery sea.

Gabriel spoke again, "Jesus favors you. He feels your pain. She will be separated from the light of God until you fulfill your quest. Remember though, if you do not slay him *with the spear*, she will return to the fire."

Relief overwhelmed me. I could sleep right

Eulogy

now, but did not long for it.

"Centurion," Ardin said to me.

"Yes," he woke me from a staring state.

"I feel fire in my throat like I've eaten sand."

"Uh oh," I had forgotten that he had not partook in the worst part of this curse yet, and neither had Thanos.

"What?"

"You must feed."

"We cannot kill our horses, and the rats will do no good," Thanos was turning out to be the life of the party, "There is only one option."

"Okay, but only if you stop when I tell you to. I will change him myself." I got the chalice. We ascended to the helm.

I sure hope Gabriel was right about this mind control thing. He would recruit better than anyone in his wanderings. Peregrine could also grant us immense advantages when it came to hiding or traveling safely. Peregrine was sleeping at the helm.

"You grab this hand, Thanos. You grab the other, Ardin. Bite into his wrists. I will hold his head if he struggles," I ordered.

They bit softly and broke his skin. He did not move. His eyes fluttered. I gently opened one eyelid to watch the veins turn less red and recede in size. Their eyes intently watching me the entire time, I waved them. I opened his mouth and fed him the chalice.

Peregrine woke the next morning, no worse for wear. He came down to us, wondering how the scars came on his wrists. We looked each other, searching for an explanation.

"Harpies came in the middle of the night," Thanos explained. "The harpies tried to steal you away. We fought them off while you slept."

Thanos was starting to become rather creative in his melancholy.

Peregrine wondered still, "Really? Hmm, I didn't think I was that well thought of by the harpies."

"They wanted your romantic sense of humor," Ardin said.

"Ha, that's great!" He ascended again to the helm chuckling all the while.

I had tested out my powers before we docked in Rome. After a moment, Peregrine came back down

CXVI

Eulogy

the stairs. He looked at us, put his hand on the floor and walked his feet up the wall. Then he released his hand and put all his weight on his head. After a moment, he dropped his feet down and stood up.

He looked at us, paused and said, "I'm sorry, I don't know why I did that," he turned, shaking his head, and went back up the stairs.

The others looked at me.

I shrugged, "Men without souls have no will." We all laughed.

We arrived at the port of Rome. We got our horses and Thanos and Ardin helped me carry Oriana into the wagon. The three of us lifted the wagon, coffin and all, up the stairs to the dock.

The package was not heavy, but awkward. I feared tipping her over out of the wagon and exposing her beauteous skin to the sea air. I ordered Peregrine to stay. He obeyed.

Thanos and Ardin anchored the wagon to the side bridles. I rode in front of them, leading them to her former village. It was on the other side of Rome in the farming district and through the forest. We walked for miles. I found the edge of the forest. We found the clearing easily. My dream guided me like a map was laid out in my very hands.

Her family had not been back. There were no smoldering shacks, no more piles of rubble: only pebbles covered in dirt and leaves. Time certainly had made its mark on this place.

There was a parting in the trees where the sun shone on the center of the clearing. We placed her there and the sun showed on her face. I picked dandelions for her and placed them on her casket. I looked at her for the longest time. Her face had not changed.

"I can't leave her!" I screamed to the sky. "How will I know she will be okay here?" What if wild dogs came and mulled her body? What if a great wind came and knocked the glass off her casket to rot her brilliant features? My brain was wild with stressful indecision.

"I have to be alone for a moment."

I went to the edge of the forest, to the wheat field. I lay down in it and closed my eyes. This was a good way to listen. I waited for the 'molding of my foot steps' as Gabriel had promised. Night came and still no answer. Three days went by; I lay there on the ground.

CXVIII

Eulogy

"*WHAT ARE YOU DOING?*" There came the lightening flash in front of me.

"I will not leave her unprotected. I was laying here to wait on your word of what to do," I explained to the glowing, growling messenger.

"*Can you not think of anything for yourself, you feeble human! I care not about your dead lover. Create a protector if you will, but make sure that he will do God's work in the process.*" He flashed away. It must be busy in Heaven. I went back to the clearing.

"Ardin, watch over Oriana until I come back."

"Are you coming back," he wondered fearfully.

"Of course my friend, that is why I am not taking you over Thanos."

Thanos wondered a look at me. I could not tell him that I would be tempted to leave him there for all eternity. His depressing expressions could not be tolerated for long. But I already knew he would be the guard of the scrolls. The chalice and Oriana would be kept watch of here.

We sat in the market place for a while. I watched and listened. In the night, I noticed glowing rings around their bodies.

A.R. Perkins

"Can you see that," I asked Thanos.

"What the aura? I can only see the red and golden ones."

"Those must be the ones to choose from, but which color is the right one?"

We noticed two, one golden, one red walking towards the dock. We followed them. They were talking with Peregrine.

"No, I cannot take you to Jerusalem until my fee comes back from his dealings in the city," Peregrine said to them. He had not seen me yet, and I raced to him in the most human way possible. I asked him to step onto the dock with me.

"Do you feel different, Peregrine?"

"Yes, Centurion, I do."

"Can you tell me, which of these to passengers appeal to you?"

"The red one, sir."

"Do you want to kill them or let them live?"

He paused for a moment and looked at me horrified.

I replied to his expression, "Do not be afraid, Peregrine. I will explain all of this later. Please look inside yourself and tell me the truth."

Eulogy

"I- I -I want to bleed him dry."

"And, what of the golden aura?"

"Let him live, but not set him free."

"Thank you, Peregrine."

Now, I knew what aura to look for in our time of need without hindering the chess match Gabriel wanted so desperately to conquer.

We waited until Peregrine proposed the innocent notion of the stay to the two 'recruits.' I walked up to the one with the golden aura.

"What's your name, son?" He was fair skinned and had green eyes. His hair was sandy blonde, like my wheat field.

"Pax," he replied.

"What an appropriate name, Pax! Do you wish to walk with me a while until our boat is ready. I need you to do me a favor. It will be the biggest decision of your life."

"Well, sir, I really have nothing better to do with my life. My family died and I am going to Jerusalem to take part in the riots. I figured that if I was going to die, I might as well do it for a cause, right?"

"What would you say if I told you, I could give

you a cause and let you live out your days? You could live up to your name, Pax."

"That would be wonderful, sir!"

"It will come at a price though."

"Anything would be better than this. I am in sorrow all the time. My heart is empty."

We walked, talking and I mounted my horse. His eyes glowed red in the night. Before Pax could notice them, I reached out to him for a boost up. We rode until we got to the clearing in silence.

"Centurion," Ardin said as he beat on his chest.

"This is your purpose now," I held my hand toward Oriana, "and this," I gave him the chalice. "You will hunt the animals of the forest. Ardin and I will return with building materials. You will have a long time to build."

"She's beautiful!" Pax awed at her face in the moon light.

"I hope to keep her that way, friend. This chalice, also, is to remains unscathed. Protect them with your life along with the family in the house by the field."

He nodded. Ardin and I came back with a wagon full of masonry and concrete mixture. We

Eulogy

left the wagon and headed off.

"What am I to hunt with?" Pax wondered, yelling to us.

We turned out heads to each other and Ardin said, "You'll figure it out." I smiled at him and shook my head downwardly.

Back on the ship, we waited until daylight to speak with Pilate. Our next mission was to seek out and the three others that shared my fate. Before we went up to the deck to casually fish, we visited Peregrine in the helm. We explained that we changed him in the middle of the night, but did not go into detail about our thirsty attack. I told him how we needed him in our mission. He took it rather well and even seemed a bit excited that he would never die. I thanked him for the advice again on the auras as well.

"This poor old ship is good for hiding and traveling but where are we going to keep them all?" Ardin wondered.

"Yeah, this ol' clinker will be rotting far before your mission is complete, Centurion," Thanos said.

The sea once calm, started to rumble. Pool rings started from the bow of the bottom of the ship to the back. We looked at each other in fear. Was it the kraken or a large whale? The wind blew front ways, then cross ways, across the whole of the ship. Peregrine in the enclosed helm, continued to sail as if nothing happened.

It started at the dirty brown pennant, which once may have been white, at the crow's nest. It turned scarlet and showed a picture of a bleeding heart with a crown of thorns surrounding it and a piercing through it: spikes driven through, three on the top. The mainmast and mainsails turned scarlet as well and depicted the same. The spars that held the masts started glistening bright silver in the moonlight and changed from termite-eaten wood into strong metal, from top to deck. The deck, of the same decrepit color turned shiny gold with diamond inlets protruding from the surface.

"We're going to sink!" Thanos left to the side to jump overboard.

"No, wait, Thanos," I said, "Was it not you that was just complaining?" I laughed.

Just then, bow to stern, it visually expanded, the color infested the ship as it grew. The helm's roof and porch deck changed to copper. The helm

glittered in gold under Peregrine's hands.

"Well!" Peregrine shouted outside the window, "not bad for an ol' ship, is it?" He laughed in delight.

The figurehead shaped from a mermaid to a wooden angel. The wings wrapped out on the sides of the bow. The face looking familiar, turned white, the eyes diamonds, the wings silver and blue- the rest of the body, clothed in gold. The banisters surrounding the ship became bronze. The whole outside of the ship turned red in cedar, then pure white. By the left angel wing, the escutcheon formed and said, "Fidelis Donec Terminus:" Faithful until the End.

We were curious to see the lastage. Our horses were enclosed in tempered glass holding, diamond sandstone under their feet. A separate door yards in front of the companionway. The room was large and empty, but for racks and chests, also empty. There stood another door to the right corner to another stairwell, down again, banisters bronzed and cedar wood steps. Around the circular stairwell to the end was the great expansion of the ship wide. Benches, row after row, of cedar, a door at the end-portholes on each side. Oars lay in front of the benches on the floor. A door at the end of the grand space had no doorknob. It could not be opened.

We ascended to the cargo hold and saw a door in behind the stair well. It held a grand cedar desk. Stationary and quills with ink bottles lay neatly there. Three kingly chairs sat, one on each side. They had velour cushions and backings in red, gold filigree for the arms and feet.

Bookshelves empty on every wall. Another door went to another large expanse of the ship- larger portholes in every window. A tall staircase went up to the dock of the ship. This room was completely cedar and only chains linked to rings in front of the portholes.

We went up to the bulwark and saw another cedar door leading underneath the helm station. We opened it to a long stretched hallway which had ten doors on each side. Each room was empty but for two pairs of steel framed twin beds and a small seating area against the back wall- one porthole above the loveseat. All rooms were identical.

We went out to the deck wondering at it all.

"I wonder," Ardin paused.

CXXVI

Eulogy

We looked at each other then we walked back down to what was now the stable.

"Tempered glass seems a strange material for horses to be stabled in," Ardin had a curious look on his face.

"I noticed last night that Marcellus' eyes were fireballs in the night. Many things are noticeable to us in the night."

"Fatality has yellow eyes and. . .Oh. . . The pupils are slanted vertically . . . like a snake's!"

"Brutus doesn't look too different, he's just red," Ardin disappointed.

"Fatality is completely light green now. He only tinged a bit under the flanks before. I don't have a horse; I have a snake in a horse's costume." Thanos seemed shocked.

Ardin opened the top part of the tempered glass and Brutus blew to wriggle his lips at him. The changes have bothered them a bit.

"It is okay, Brutus" Ardin said softly and patted him. I did the same for my steed.

Brutus let out a wild nay. His eyes were flames of red fire; the fur on his hooves ignited and turned to the hooves a glowing red. His tail and mane flashed tongues of red to yellow from root to end. Tiny flames also came out his nose when breathing out.

"Wow! My horse is awesome!"

When I patted Marcellus, fires glowing, hooves scarlet, the tail and mane braided itself close to the skin. We heard a crashing, bumping sound in the empty rack room- then, another loud *thurump* on the deck. We inspected the room and all the racks were full of flails, bo's, daggers, sai's, swords, bisarmes, three-sectioned-staffs, spears, halberds, glaives, and morning stars. The Chests were full of helmets, methril, chain mail, gauntlets, and sheathes for both shins and wrists.

"You haven't touched Fatality yet, Thanos," I reminded.

We left the Armory and Thanos visited Fatality. His tail and mane disappeared. His fur, where Thanos touched him, turned into green scales, hard as stone. His entire body transformed into them from the contact point. Tiny nubs appeared under his shoulder blades. They exponentially grew out, scales and leather-like material. Moments went by, two brown-green wings stretched, then folded onto

Eulogy

the sides. Fatality's breath was a fog of green that bothered our sinuses. The saddles were hung on the far wall by the door. Thanos' saddle transformed its shape.

"Well, at least something good came out of this immortality," Thanos thought out loud.

I was glad to see him in higher spirits.

We went to the huge hull underneath the deck to view two rows of molten lava and rock cannons. Metal baskets held cannonballs of fire. The chains that held them were not charred. The floor beneath them stayed intact. The floor changed from wood to black diamond sandstone.

It was morning; we went to the census report first. Issachar, Matthias and Gad were not at the residence listed. I went to Pilate. I saluted him in Roman fashion.

"I request audience with you, sir, if not to indispose."

"You are never a disposition, Centurion."

"Where are Issachar, Matthias, and Gad stationed?"

"Well, some rather evil phenomena have been attacking them after the death of the King of the

Jews. I separated them to different stations about the empire. They truly feared for their lives, Centurion. I hope you find them and protect them. Issachar is in Tyre, Matthias is in Joppa, and Gad is in Ezion Geber."

"I will, Pilate. Thank you for the information."

I saluted again and returned for the Lieutenants.

"First we head to Joppa."

CXXX

Then he said to them all: "If anyone would come after me, he must deny himself and take up his cross daily and follow me. For whoever wants to save his life will lose it, but whoever loses his life for me will save it. What good is it for a man to gain the whole world and lose his soul?"   - Luke 9: 23-25

Pursuit

In the daylight, our steeds were relatively normal looking, but for Fatality and his strange tone. Brutus looked fawn colored in the light. We left the boat and traveled along the North-western road toward the coast.

Matthias was in the marketplace buying many barrels of wine.

I walked to him softly and pulled his arm around his shoulder, "Hi! Remember me?"

He looked at me eyes wide. Ardin and Thanos put the last barrel in his wagon. We bought enough food for Matthias for the week's trip. Ardin tugged the load behind him. Thanos mounted his horse, dragging Brutus behind.

"We *do* have a hitch, you know Ardin," Thanos razzed. Ardin laughed to himself, "Are you green in more ways than one, Thanos?"

Thanos growled at him and his eyes changed saffron as he stared.

"STOP IT, you *two*." This mind order kept the peace.   I   did   this   often.

We headed toward Jerusalem, then back to the port. I bolted the door with Matthias and his perishables inside the lodging. We sailed the boat down the river to the Mediterranean Sea and sailed North to Tyre.

In Tyre, Issachar's residence was on the highest hill in the city with a viewpoint of the coast. It was white marble throughout with gold trim. I believed I may need some assistance with this so; *we* rode up the exaggerated concrete stairs, dismounted and pounded on his door. He opened it slowly a small crack and then closed it quickly. Ardin and I took sides of the large cedar door and kicked it simultaneously.

"No, NO! Don't let them in here! Get out or they will torture you as well!" Issachar was rambling about the evil Pilate warned us about.

"Soldier, we will share the same fate, but not as you are thinking. Restrain him!"

Ardin tied his wrists and took him to his steed. He threw him up in the saddle with ease. Issachar's eyes were fearful and he covered them in Brutus' mane.

"Gather his belongings and pack them in bed sheets. I'm sure he will want them where he's going. Don't forget the gold," I ordered.

Ardin and Thanos went to work and strapped six half-man sized bundles, two on each horse.

"Thank you, you did not have to do that, I don't deserve such kindness."

"We will protect you and take care of you, but there is only one way for *you* to truly serve. You *will* share our fate. Let's go.

I hated to have to bind him and I was not going to drag him down the stories of stairs. My mission was clear, but my empathy was unmasked for this creature. Regardless of his lifestyle, he was happy to leave it to escape the fear.

He smiled calmly and rested his head in slumber. I knew that kind of peace once. Watching him, I envied him. Back at The Fidelis, Ardin grabbed him and carried like a child to his room. Thanos and I quietly put his belongings in his room. I did not bother to bolt the door.

The final stop was the long and tumultuous trek

to Gad. With our missions so new and no tactics of war decided, I did not trust anyone to protect the captives but Ardin and myself. Ardin and I were joined at the hip, so we went to Ezion Geber by sea and through the Nile River. The Great Pyramids and the Sphinx were on the way. We recruited some as we saw the sites. In the daylight, their auras were invisible. We took no women, for none of us were ready for that decision quite yet. There was only one that I would change if I could.

We bought more food from the market place and loaded it into the cargo hold. Matthias had enough wine for all fifteen of my newly acquired friends, and then some. The men were in awe of the mighty galleon, and settled right in, sharing rooms. We made a large table out of five smaller oak tables on the deck and bolted each section down. The men ate and we chatted about their lives until the sun set. They were weary and many retreated to their previously claimed quarters.

I discussed the pursuit of Gad with Peregrine.

"It's going to be tough getting to Ezion Geber by sea," he explained. "The Nile does not have any tributaries that flow into the Red Sea. The only way

to get there is to go all the way around. You'd think some people would get together with some shovels and start digging." He laughed at the thought. "There is a tributary that will get us close called the Gebel Gharib out of Qena, but we'll have to backtrack north again. There's about ten miles of land between us, even after we cross the separations. This galleon is enormous and your horses won't be able to gain traction in the sand, no matter how gifted they may be."

I looked at him for the longest time in distressed confusion. Had I taken this controlling state to a degree that caused mishap? I saw no other option and I was going not to leave. I was the Centurion.

"Stay the course. Sail to Qena and the lieutenants and I will discuss our next action."

"Whatever you say; it seems like a big waste of time to me."

"What do we have, but time, Peregrine."

He smiled slyly at me. "That we do, sir. That . . . we . . . do."

Ardin was in the armory testing out his flail.

"Hey, look at this," he wondered at me.

I went over to the flail as he showed me the

grip. There was an etched symbol in the diamond handle. It was a triangle with the point at the top and the flat on the bottom, a line from the point to the middle of the bottom line, and a circle within it. The name written vertically in Arabic: 'Israfel, angel of blaze.' When Ardin swung the flail, the ball inflamed and grew larger. The chain, impermeable, extended with his whip. I ducked toward the door. This powerful weapon could surely even harm those such as me. I interrupted Ardin's demonstration, which he found much satisfaction in, and he placed the mystic carnage maker onto its space on the wall. We left and looked for Thanos.

We searched every room, stern to bow, helm to cargo hold. Thanos was inevitably in the last place we looked. He was on the row deck, standing pensively at the inoperable door.

"We need not worry about that right now, Thanos," I interjected. "We have more important things to discuss."

"This room perturbs me. What is its purpose? I have come to the realization that, everything in this life, immortal or not, has a purpose, why not this?"

"I'm sure it will come with time, Thanos. Let's ascend to the fore cabin."

"Do we need these oars for something? Are we to enslave those we've changed for *that* purpose?"

We all stopped at this question, it was a good one.

"No, Thanos, I would not expect those we've changed to serve in that manner. That is not the purpose of this curse."

We paused, Thanos, grunted disconcerted, and began the ascent. We followed.

"Peregrine says we are unable to get to Ezion Geber by sea. He states that there is a tributary that will not connect to the Red Sea and he will have to backtrack upstream. I was thinking he could sail as much as he could and we could push the boat across the sand at night, while the mortals slept, but he says there is no way to gain enough traction in the sand. Do any of you have suggestions?"

"Why don't we just go get him? Why did we have to go around and through the Nile like this? This makes no sense," Thanos grunted.

"This was the way I was compelled to go, Thanos. The new recruits are not changed and we

cannot risk the secrecy if the changed we've recruited prior become thirsty. I have a bit of trouble trusting Peregrine with this. He is not a soldier. Only my mind ordering gift and Ardin's strength could restrain them."

"If only we could fly. Then this wouldn't be an issue," Ardin mentioned.

"That would *definitely* cause some suspicion," I laughed.

"We could do it at night," Ardin remarked.

I shook my head, "Too hard to hide this galleon. We cannot ask Gabriel to do this, he will refuse. He knows this risk too."

"So . . . make it invisible," Ardin laughed robustly.

We all laughed too. God's powers could do amazing things, but if this was the plan he compelled for us, he would have done this already.

"Perhaps it is simply my worry that is causing this, but we need to keep a watchful eye on the recruits, and we *need* to get to Gad.

We were all quiet for a moment.

Ardin spoke first, "Well, if that's the case, and you say *'my strength'* is the only thing that can

A.R. Perkins

restrain them' we should separate them. We should wait for night, view their auras and see who needs to be paired up. Then we change the selected few. We make up a story that they became ill and died. We had to bury them in the sand. We put them in the stockade and dump their bodies at night once we are in open water."

"That is disgusting, Ardin!" Thanos repulsed, "their bodies will wreak."

"Do you have a better suggestion?"

"Well," I thought, "they *do* need to be changed eventually. We will do it before we get to Jerusalem. Issachar and Matthias are charged to protect Mary, Jesus' mother. For now we need to uphold discretion. Your story will do well, Ardin, when that time comes. There are plenty of rooms though. Even though they are comfortable, we could separate the auras to their own rooms and pair them later, or order them to feed on the one's I say. For now, we *need* to demise how to get to Gad," I redirected.

"Well, when I touched Fatality, he grew wings. I wonder if I touched your steeds if they will do the same." Thanos had a good idea.

"Let's go see," I said.

We opened the door to the stable and Thanos patted Marcellus first. A large eight foot long scythe materialized and floated in mid-air beside him. Samael's name was on this one. The symbol was an E with circles and curves on the ends. The inscriptions were not on the black handle though, but on the three foot angular blade.

"Well, *that* was not what I expected," Thanos jeered. "Wow! This could really do some damage!"

He grabbed it and his clothes became a black hooded robe that covered all but his toes.

"You're scary lookin,' Thanos," Ardin amazed.

"Okay, so that didn't do like we thought it would."

Thanos patted Ardin's steed, the scythe's blade flamed in a glowing bright green. The longer he patted, the more the flame grew. It was all over his body but did not burn the robe. His flesh was no more and his bones were exposed. His eyes glowed red flame. We backed away from him.

"Release the horse! Thanos, Let go!!!"

His fiery eyes looked toward me- a raspy voice

that came from the lips that were no more asked, "Why?"

Ardin ran at him and tackled him to the ground. After a few moments, Thanos returned to his former self. It was early in the day.

"You should have seen yourself, Thanos. You should stay in the quarters at night until the mortals are changed. You scared us to death!"

"That is what I am," he replied.

"Well, just the same. Please do this, do not make me order you to." I hated having to control him.

"Well, now that *that's* an unexpected change of events," Ardin said in horror, "there is no way *he* can go and get Gad. The way we found Issachar and Matthias, the site of Thanos would keel Gad over dead."

"No, but his horse can. I have an idea." I opened Fatality's pen, careful not to touch his skin. I took him up to the deck. I hoped this would work. I made certain all crew were in their quarters. They slept until the sun was high in the sky.

While the coast was clear; I stood Fatality in the center on the deck. Thanos and Ardin stood by the

helm deck and watched curiously. Here we go, I thought to myself. I put both my hands on Fatality's neck sides and rubbed. The horse whinnied and stomped his foot. I kept rubbing. From his chest to his flanks he grew. His neck stretched taller. I was rubbing his neck, then his chest, then his legs, until his hooves were large giants in front of me. This was not what I expected.

"Thanos! Ardin!" I called.

Thanos patted the right hind ankle, "Sit, Fatality!" The steed obeyed. Thanos on the right, Ardin on the left hand, I at the chest patted circularly. The fur turned to emerald scales as it did before, the mail and tail disappeared, the hooves became claws and wings stretched upward then folded. When he breathed, it was no longer gaseous fumes, but flames, like Ardin's horse. The ship grew again. I knew the pen would be larger before I looked to confirm it. I doubted the tempered glass would hold him though, but there wasn't time. We stopped the caress and stood back to view the monster we had made. He was beautiful!

"No," Thanos said to Fatality, "it is okay. We need you in this shape to rescue a friend."

A.R. Perkins

"You can hear him?" Ardin asked.

"Yes, he asked what was going on and if he was a monster" Thanos chuckled.

"He will return to normal when it is of need. Look the ship has grown to hold his weight and to create a new holding for him," I mentioned for them to notice, too.

"Amazing," Ardin explained.

The steps to the stable were no longer wood but the diamond sandstone as the floor in the gunnage room and the stairwell was ten times the width it was. The pens were moved to the back of the stable. Chains and three large collars were attached to the marble walls. The whole of the stable was one forth the size of the galleon.

"I will leave tonight with Fatality. Ardin will set up the feast as usually for the crew. Thanos, you must think up a way to get us some oar men. That is your mission for now.

When all the crew was asleep, Thanos explained to Fatality in further detail. I did not want to ride the beast without his permission that may become a deadly undertaking. Thanos strapped on the harness in between his wings. His fingers looked fragile, as

they turned into bone after dusk, but they had all the strength he did in the sunlight.

"How do you feel about your new face, Thanos?" Ardin looked concerned. His growl replied as his burning sockets moved in his direction, "I feel powerful in this shape. Perhaps, this is my mission. I feel a tugging on this ship toward some of the crew. I know they are about to die."

I saw the hair stand up on Ardin's arm and neck and asked, "Does he scare you now, Ardin?"

"A bit," He laughed loudly, "I know we have nothing to fear from him, but I pity the mortals that may see his face."

"Does Fatality understand, Thanos?"

"Yes, he gives permission for you to ride. I explained to him that you cannot communicate with him as I do. He only asks that you do not pull his reins too hard, just a nudge will do."

I nodded. "Thank you, Fatality."

"He says he's 'glad to help, '" Thanos translated. Fatality's snake-like eyes turned as soft as they could while looking at me. His mouth curled upward showing his immense sharp fangs,

just a few, though. It was a kind smile, as dragons go.

The ship continued on the stream upward as we traveled on the tributary Peregrine had mentioned. I felt the need to leave for Gad as soon as possible. I told Peregrine to continue until there was no stream left and wait for me. He nodded and was in awe of the beast. He seemed a sheltered man. All his travels had taught him temperance. Even in his new life, he seemed *very* human and understanding.

Fatality ducked his head and lifted his massive paw as a prop. I patted his neck in gratitude, looked at him compassionately, and smiled. I put my hand on his paw to hoist myself up, straddled his neck, and scooted downward into the special saddle. I belted myself in, *very tightly*. As much as I trusted the beast, I was not a big fan of flying. I inhaled deeply, looked at Thanos, and nodded. The fear was evident in my eyes. I let out the breath that filled my lungs to the brim, and Thanos looked at Fatality and nodded. He stood and the leather wings began to flap. My hair tousled in the breeze it created. My eyes became as dry as desert boulders. I blinked quite a bit from the whirl.

Once we were in the air, the breeze subsided from the sides of him and concentrated towards the front. We flew very high above the clouds until we could see no more land. Fatality shot downward. My heart leaped into my throat. If it beat in my chest it would have skipped or stopped all together.

I leaned forward and whispered, "Let's not do that again, please, Fatality."

His eyes moved sideways to my face and the smile returned. He must be apologizing. This was his first flight too though. He was enthralled with it. He flew just above the sea and opened his mouth a bit. His claws grazed across it. The he flew up again until we found land. It took only a fragment of time to get there.

I searched the camp. The men slept soundly. In all twelve tents, there was not a sign of Gad. I felt compelled to search East over the mountain range. I found him hiding in a cave by the Abarim Mountains. He was shivering in a hole though it was a good eighty-five degrees in the night. I ran to him and knelt in the sand in front of him. His eyes were wild and his head was flailing back and forth. He was gasping every time he looked around

him.

I grabbed his arm and shook him out of his frightened state. He looked at me and fell his head to my chest and cried.

"Come on, its okay now. You will be protected."

I took the wine skin mixed with my blood and let him drink. I heard his heart stop, he calmed instantly after that.

"I believed what you said, Centurion. 'Truly this man was the son of God.' I believed on him right then. I regretted killing Him. I *hurt* Him!"

He started to cry again.

"You have a purpose now. The evil will not bother you again. I know you regret; I do too. But we, who share the same curse, will make it up to Him. You are to help me to defeat the Fallen Angel in flesh and protect the relics of Jesus, the one we slain."

"I will do anything for Him and you. Thank you for this cursed gift. It is better than hiding in this hole." He laughed a bit, and then picked himself up. I assisted.

I summoned Gabriel. His eyes were calm.

CL

"Archangel, what is this evil that torments them so?"

"Wraiths of regret: now that he is changed, he will fear them no more. This one though, is the one exception to the rule."

"I don't understand."

"Your souls were tarnished and you are cursed because you did not believe. You had to gain immortality through your works. Your encased souls are the sign of the end. His soul must now wait until Lucifer is slain to see the benefits of his afterlife."

I felt terrible in that instant. I didn't realize.

Gad looked up at him and smiled grandly. His reaction was quite different from Peregrine's.

Gabriel ordered, "Touch your steed, Centurion. We will be sure Gad will never fear again."

I did so and a scimitar, with a pearl engraved handle fell to the sand in front of Gad's feet. The engravings were blue sapphire lightning bolts. A symbol was etched in the handle. It was a three, faced toward the left, with a curve on the bottom that squiggled angularly into a lightening shape. Tiny circles with on each point. The Arabic name

of Barakial was vertically etched below. A stallion walked from behind the cliff. It was silver, with a dark gray main and tail, and light grey eyes.

"You, Centurion, are to take the river back to Jerusalem. Gad, I know this is difficult for you, but your journey will lead you North across the desert. You must recruit scribes along the way. Only hunt at night. Do not feed on the white auras, for they will share your fate or die."

Gad looked confused.

"It is part of the curse, Gad. I feel great regret, but now you will be safe. Your purpose now is to aid in the protection of the scrolls. You must feed on human blood to survive in your immortality. This is what Gabriel is explaining."

"Yes that is what I am saying. You have come to interpret angelic verbiage well, Centurion," a bell like chime came from his opened mouth.

"We are bonded, correct?"

"We cannot be so forever. There will be a time when you may experience my silence."

This greatly saddened me.

"Fear not, Centurion, no matter what, you will be provided for. Ramiel has given you a gift. It lay

on your fore cabin desk. With your astuteness in other languages, I'm positive you will be able to decipher it. It can only be written in Arabic, for it is the language of God."

"Thank him for me, Gabriel."

"Selaphiel has before you even spoke it. He attuned to your prayer and humble gratitude."

I was in awe of this powerful communication between the angels and myself.

"All humankind is linked to us in this manner; some are too blind to take notice." He was saddened at this thought. He did not mention the things I knew he noticed of our mission. It was difficult to know what he was thinking, though we were bonded, not by the mind. He gave instruction through my angst, not like speaking whispers within my head.

He looked at me proudly.

"Your beast is impressive."

"This is Fatality."

"Yes, I know. Change the others into the like. They will be powerful forces in battle. At the dawn of the third day, they will be able to transform into their former shapes and you can change them at

will. The word will be 'Merkabah,' for it is the chariot of God."

This was much easier than rubbing them for several minutes. That would be a huge inconvenience in a crisis.

"Go, now and take the scribes to the caves. Gad and others will protect them there. Issachar and Matthias must pursue their mission as well. You must change the recruits you acquired. The Mary's and John the beloved are in danger. The disciples will be martyred as well without your protection. The Holy Spirit is in them, but you are the spirit in the flesh with all the fervor it possesses."

I nodded to him, until next time, I thought.

"Do not fear Fatality. He is a miracle, Gad. Besides, you do not have to fear death anymore. We can change your stallion as well if you wish, Ardin and me.

"He's marvelous!"

"You ready to go, Fatality?"

He looked at me, bowed his head, and raised his paw as before. I mounted.

"See you in Jerusalem, Gad."

It was almost morning, the moon was setting

and the darkness shaded blue in the horizon. I feared the worst as we crossed the sea. I gulped and the anxiety made me grip the reins until my knuckles turned white. Fatality felt it too. I felt the muscles under my legs tighten and he flapped his wings faster.

Moments past and the scales on his head turned to fur again. Green hair started to grow. I could see the sliver shining in the horizon. Fatality whinnied and flapped so fast I could not see his wings any more. He descended slowly near the water as before. Then, suddenly we were covered with water. I swam off Fatality and grabbed his reins. A mortal would have been carried under by his weight. I pulled with all my might until he was beside me. We swam to the surface and moved our appendages to shore.

"Well that was close. Can you breathe under water? I don't know, but I wasn't going to test it."

He looked at me, his eyebrows downward. I did not understand his horse like expression.

"Well, Thanos will have to tell me I suppose."

He shook from head and wobbled his back hooves a bit with the force.

"Do you need to rest?"

Fatality walked towards a cactus, stopped, and looked back at me. I cut it down and shaved off the needles with my hands. He ate it. He must not be able to breathe underwater if he had to eat.

"Okay, you ready?"

He sat down and the same look was given. He reminded me of Thanos in the old days. I wished he was a dragon again. I sat across from him in the sand, "Just let me know."

The sun was forty degrees in the sky when he rose up. We walked beside each other in the sand.

"I will walk with you, Fatality. I know you've done enough. I guess you're pretty mad about Gad's quest. We didn't take him with us, but we *did* rescue him. He would not have been able to fulfill his mission if we hadn't gone."

He looked at me this time with kinder eyes, and I knew he understood now.

The sun was setting in the sky by the time we reached the boat.

"What have you done to my horse? I could hear his moping miles away!" Thanos' eyes gleamed with flame though he was human like for now. He

came down the dock and took Fatality's reins when shooting the flames through me.

"I'm sorry, Thanos. We didn't quite make it over the sea in time and he nearly drowned when we fell into the sea.

"Drown? My horse can't drown, he just hates water."

"Well, I was concerned about that and I thought, since he ate, that he was mortal."

"Do we not *eat?*"

He *did* have a point. He gestures to Fatality and nudged his reins. The steed followed *very* willingly, almost trotting to the stable. I ran after Thanos.

"Did you find out a way to create some oar men?"

He laughed out loud, "O YES! But I will let Ardin tell you about that. They are in the orlop. I will take care of them once the sun goes down." He laughed as he walked fatality to the stable.

I went up to the helm dock where Peregrine was sitting.

"Where is your rescue, Centurion," he asked with a curious look.

A.R. Perkins

"He was given another mission by land; we will meet up with him in Jerusalem. That is our next stop. Where's Ardin, I was told I need to discuss something with him?"

"Um . . . yes," Peregrine looked worried. "He's in your fore cabin."

I passed by Thanos and Fatality on the way. Thanos was stroking him and shushing him comforting, "It's all over now."

Poor thing, I really don't understand how melancholy a horse could be about taking a bath, especially if he couldn't die.

I saw Ardin at the large desk in the head chair. His forehead was in his hands.

"I'm sorry, friend. I tried to stop them."

"What *are* you talking about, Ardin?"

"One of the older recruits got thirsty. He started to bite one of his roommates. The others were horrified and started to scream. I ran from the bow where I was fishing to the commotion, but I was too late. Our discretion was compromised. I don't know how many of the reds found out, because I didn't think before I acted."

"*What did you do, Ardin!!!?*" I understood

peregrine's expression now, and Thanos' dark laughter.

"I separated as many of the yellows as I could. I forced them to drink the wine we have concocted for the change. I told them it would save them from the monster. Then I bolted their door. I took the other that heard it, all of them into the room with the changed ones and bolted them in. They are all dead."

"All of them," I asked.

"I assume so. All I've heard was screaming and talking through the door about 'what they have become.'" He put his head back in his hands and shook his head. "I think Thanos had the gall to poke his head in and order them to drag the bodies downstairs. I haven't spoken with him since I bolted the door and came in here. I heard thumping down the stairs after a long silence."

I went down to the orlop. Thanos was standing over the bodies. He had cut his wrist with his scythe. When they awoke, he motioned them to the benches. Mundanely, they rowed and took orders to stop.

CLIX

A.R. Perkins

"Wonderful, Centurion, your slaves!"

I looked at him in shock. This was *wrong*. How could he feel so about this?

"They are your charge, Thanos. I want no part of this."

"Gladly," he bowed to me.

His face would be hidden from view, our discretion was salvaged, and our boat was faster. I left the orlop and searched for survivors. There were none, just as Ardin had feared.

"I want every man on deck *RIGHT NOW!!!*"

The men ran dressing themselves like pirates during a brigade. I summoned Gabriel to the table as well. I sat at the head and the others sat after.

"I want everyone to understand something." I looked at each of them. "I assumed that, because you were changed, you knew your purpose. We had discussed this after your hearts had stopped. I want to know the one responsible for this."

Ardin spoke, "It was Marcus, sir."

"Thank you, Lieutenant."

Gabriel interjected as I opened to speak.

"The punishment for releasing our discretion is the ability to die. Consider this morning your last sunrise, for the purity of the sun will burn your flesh to ash from outside to your very core. Rosalba no longer holds your soul; it is now encased in the key to Hell, never to be released. Your existence is void. Holy water and bane venom are now your weaknesses. You will not fight alongside your brothers. You will only live for death. Take him to the orlop to row with your un-dead, for he is now a slave to the night."

Marcus looked at us in repentant fright. He started to get up and gestured to flash across the boat's edge. Thanos grabbed him in that instant and took him down the stairs. No one dared to cross his frightening glare.

"Gabriel?" I asked. He looked at me, his face softened.

"I apologize whole-heartedly for this. I left Ardin in charge."

"Men make mistakes. All is forgiven. Now you have your rowers and the discretion is upheld. Know this, centurion; you are witness to the Almighty's power when His son was sacrificed. There is no one that cannot be saved. Humanity was kiln a jar of clay by the hand of God. The

contents within mold the identity of the auras you see.

"Ardin," Gabriel looked at him, Ardin glanced up for only a moment, then down in sorrow. "You and Thanos now have the gift to mind order the men you have changed and the others when he is not around. Use it wisely and do not neglect nor take advantage of it. We will be watching."

"WAIT! Gabriel, do not leave!" I yelled.

"Yes, you have another question?"

"Gabriel," I paused again and stuttered, "I- is there nothing you can do for Oriana?"

"Ah . . . I wondered when you were going to bring that up, *again*." He, chuckling, a tiny bell, paused.

"Well *you said* 'there is no one that cannot be saved.'"

"That is correct."

"What if you brought her back to me in *this* life?"

"I will have to take that up with Metatron and Azrael, but her existence would not be the same as yours. She would not completely understand this life as you do. She would live with so much regret,

she would want to die, and we would let her. Even now, she thinks of the life she could've had with you and her child."

"Why would you *'let her die?'*

"Once a name is written in the book of life and death, it *can* be erased, but the imprint remains. Once a body breathes no life, no purpose, it is destined to die again."

"I would gladly sacrifice my life for hers. If I could have been saved in my former existence, I would be now."

"Now you understand, Centurion. Unfortunately, her life ended before the sacrifice was made to purge her soul."

"I regret," I said solemnly.

"Angel's do as well, but not in the same way. I empathize with you, Centurion, but she would be no more than the un-dead you hold rowing your boat. Her fetus is dead as well."

"GOD!!!" I gripped my knuckles white against my cheekbones down to my chin. "Must you always remind me of the *obvious*, so *coldly*, so *bitterly*? FLASH AWAY, before I get my *spear!"*

He did. The men looked at me, in fear. I

CLXIII

looked weak to them at that moment, I knew I did. I wished I could cry, to feel the pain easing up in my head as the tears fought inside there. I felt nothing physical, only in the heart I once had, the soul I once had. I was nothing without her, I am nothing at all. Was I really no different from the un-dead Thanos governed?

"WHAT ARE *YOU* LOOKING AT!?" I left and descended to Marcellus.

Ardin came down with me after a while.

"Let's go on into the fore cabin and talk a bit," I said. He followed hesitantly.

"I couldn't stop them!"

"I know you can now, though. Marcus is truly cursed though now. I hope Thanos puts him in the shaded part of the boat. He is his responsibility now. This is Peregrine's boat, but all the men follow me. I should've never left. I take the blame for everything. Do not fret, Ardin. Gabriel has taken care of this issue. He told me though that there will be a time when there will be silence between us. As we sat at the desk, I picked up the gift Ramiel had given to me. The book was enormous! It was full of medieval Aramaic. The

symbols on the front spelled out <u>The Zohar</u>. This would be a good read in times at sea, where silence was my only friend.

"Let us go up top with Brutus and Marcellus. I wonder if we would need Thanos to transform the beasts."

"If he will, we will ask for him when he is done with the un-dead."

"Cleanse me hyssop, and I will be clean; wash me and I will we whiter than snow."   - Psalm 51: 7

Tempered & Forged

We arrived in Jerusalem. Issachar and Matthias researched their charge in the Census and went to her home. Gad arrived in a fright.

"We were traveling through the desert, all of us. I knew I had to keep them alive. I saw a dark shape forming in the distance approaching us with speed. A few moments later, I saw a raven black steed, fireballs for eyes. The mount was a creature with a lion's head and monkey paws holding the reins. The snake-like body wrapped around the belly of the steed. The stirrups were filled with eagle talons. The voice growled at me.

'I am here to take back what is mine.'

I knew in that instant that he was a demon and in one fail swoop, I took the sword of lightening and cut both his and the steeds head off. They fell to dust into the sand.

I knew he wanted the scribes for himself and to use them to write the scrolls in whatever way he saw fit."

Our eyes were wide and motionless as we heard Gad tell his story. We were afraid.

A.R. Perkins

"Then, we all must go in formation to the desert caves to protect the scribes."

Every venture to land presented a new trip to the marketplace. Though we only feasted by other means, we had to maintain perishables for those we protected. Our journey was not terribly long, but based on Gad's interpretation, the peril may be great. Our new bodies felt no tire from the heat. We loaded up the wagons, made our way to the Quorum, discussed our purpose, and relayed the danger of their inaction. Their eyes wide with precognition- they packed up and followed immediately thereafter.

I led the formation, Thanos on the left and Ardin on my right and trailing. Gad tailed the circle as the others surrounded the scribes. The wagon was hitched to the Quorum leader's horse. Watchful and suspicious- I noticed every flying sand grain and flicker of dust. The heat before us solidified into its own personal waves. The older scribes chose to ride with their papyrus, while the other, younger and robust prodigies walked on the outside, making an inner circle of protection.

We traveled silently for many miles. The scribes would murmur a bit, nothing I was particularly interested in. I was a soldier, not obsessed with syntax and prose, or whatever else they were discussing that made no sense to me. The others paced gracefully. I remained constant in my deliberation; I was interrupted by a high pitched sound from a few yards behind us. Gad had whistled my attention; the unchanged steeds seemed startled by it. Our three only turned their ears in aggravation.

The heat- impervious to our eternal shielding, all essence of humanity was fading into memory. I turned to Gad's whistling and saw the tight enclosing of the treasures had widened as we sauntered. I troubled to empathize for our human companions.

"Should we rest?"

We left early to avoid the impossibility of this barren wasteland. We almost made it before the fall as we approached the Jordan, few miles remaining to the caves. The younger and the Egyptian scribes dove chest and neck first into the refreshment. They cupped their hands into bucket pouring over

head, cheeks, neck and to open the parched mouths. Travelers rested also on the beach. All manner of beastly transportation sustained their primal needs.

We dismounted, filled our extra bottles and shared this with the elders that traveled in the wagon. We thought nothing of ourselves, for we didn't need to, surely they could not see we were normal. Hoping to deter the suspicion, I made a mental note to write rules to pass down and maintain our secrecy. We sat on the shoreline staggering our alignment. Gad sat beside me on the left, Ardin to my right hand side as always.

"I feel the presents of spirits here," Gad looked at me after moments of un-needed rest.

"Are they still here?"

"They are not evil, centurion. I feel a flame emitting peace. The essence is rising in me- from crown to toe. It ignites my tendons into motion and my speech to testify."

He said this, but remained stationary- knees upward at his chest, feet to his thighs, arms hugging knees, and folded hands.

"Wraiths were here at one time. Their motivations: to destroy this testimony. The history

Eulogy

behind this ancient river is *inspirational*."

I enjoyed the change his face made at the feeling he experienced. Gad was a good conversationalist. I looked forward, full of thought, to empathize with his feelings. I did not share the enchantment he was blessed with.

"This is Nen," Gad waved his hand towards his left side as he spoke. "He was the leader of the three scribes I was hard pressed to recruit."

I leaned forward and across Gad to offer my hand to him, and he looked at me curiously. I raised my eyes from my hand and met his eyes with mine. He nodded his head down and my hand descended, my stature returned. I took no offense to this. With my experience, I knew that many cultures believe it unlucky to make contact with strangers.

He seemed a timid sort of young man. Egyptian yet African as well- his hair was long and coiled in sections and his eyes were the deepest brown I had ever seen. The pupils and irises were bright, yet the whites seemed glazed over in thought. After resting by the shore side and watching the entertainment of the others relishing the water, I became extremely curious about him. He wore beadier in his locks of different shades of off white and brown. He wore abalone shell jewelry and deerskin clothing, much like Oriana's tribe.

His close proximity to me made me aware that he had been changed by Gad. Our smell was as quartz and skin molded like marble. Mortals may not notice so much, they would only see this as toned mass. Our senses were heightened. Immortality changed our view- everything was in slower motion then in mortality. Tiny things were immense. Our motions habitually slow, could speed to invisibility at the thought and movement we desired.

Whether or not the others would notice, we would not know or test, for our discretion, as always, was a priority. The soldiers saw me as a broken record in regards to this, but, I would be sure, for all time, they would not forget. It has even been drummed into the head of Marcus, though he was not allowed the opportunity to disclose what he was. Why would he want to at any rate? It would be a travesty. He was able to die, and blood drinking murderous monsters would not last long in

Eulogy

the real world.

Our world was real, but to an extent, and only to us. That, aspect of it, I think very loosely. We were created diligent insomniacs, protecting at all times, but this afterlife was a never ending nightmare. Sorrow from memories haunted me as I sat still beside that shoreline- my Oriana, living forever in my mind. I needed a distraction, so the curiosity overtook me again.

"Nen," he returned my gaze, "tell me about your mortal life. What mindset sought you to become like us?"

As he looked at me, his eyes less pensive then before, for he was thinking of this very thing, before I requested he speak it out loud. He took a breath to speak, and paused to look to the sand.

"It will be alright, Nen," Gad soothed.

The timid youngster shook his right wrist, adjusting the abalone shell bracelet habitually, then summoned the courage, and inhaled to speak.

"My mother and father were leaders of a tiny sect near Cairo. They raised my sister and me frugally. We partook in the field work by the Nile with the rest of the tribe. We were one with them though we were richer than the rest.

A terrible fire came. Our huts were destroyed. Our livestock and harvest: stolen. We always feared the neighboring tribes would see our plenty and attempt to acquire it. Unfortunately, our prophetess foresaw this plight. She gave us a hope, though, in the aftermath. She said that a virgin would bring us salvation and prosperity again.

One day soon after, the pharaoh had passed through our land casually reviewing the countryside. He peeked through his manned chariot curtain to take sight of my sister. He stopped and had his servant approach her with the proposal.

Regardless of his interest in her, he wanted a great dowry from my parents. He promised to keep her safe in his pyramid and to grant our village peace and prosperity. The irony of this was that he would destroy all of us if she was not at his quarters by dusk. She was afraid, for she did not want defiled for the sake of her tribes safety, only for the sake of true love. Silly, girl, only thirteen years of age and she cared too much for herself then for us and the greater good.

Mother dressed her in white and escorted her to

Eulogy

the palace well before the time, but she diverted the servants and ran back to us in tears. During the night, we hid in the desert. His army tracked all of us down and the entire tribe were slaughtered, my family included. I ran and hid away from their wrath. Gad found me within the caves with these scribes."

I took in his testimony with sorrow and empathy. "I'm so sorry this happened to you, Nen.

Through every   adversity comes prosperity. I myself have experienced loss and sorrow. We will take care of you until your niche is discovered in your new life."

Gad smiled at me for he knew this to be factual, Nen on the other hand retreated to his pensive state. The mortals lay floating in the Jordan for a bit, relaxing. We remained still- our minds the only muscle working sporadically.

The sun seemed to pass through the sky as a slug moves across a fallen tree branch. The others ceased their fun, sat along the shoreline, feet from us, with the wagon- their clothes already dry, waiting and wondering when we would move.

A.R. Perkins

Thanos came and whispered in my ear, "They grow suspicious of why we are still here, centurion. I feel the tension of their emotions. We must get moving."

Why is it, all the other had powers but me. Surely my 'loyalty and passion' as Gabriel had mentioned were not the only thing I had to offer to this new not life. I became somewhat annoyed with the new feeling, and thought quickly how to cross the river without cause for another reason of suspicion.

"All right then, take the wheels off the wagon and place them with in. The elders can ride our horses. Gad, you lead the steeds across the river first at the shallowest part. Then bring them back for us. We will ride, carrying the wagon corners in alignment of the beasts."

He obeyed, and we crossed the river based upon the new plan. We continued on in the same formation as before. We could see the caves in the distance and started to head toward them, after replacing the wheels of the wagon. The scribes seemed refreshed but spoke among themselves at how far left we had to travel. Could they really not

Eulogy

see the caves right in front of us?

Gad answered them, "Seven miles remain."

I nudged Marcellus closer to Gad, and leaned to ask, "Can you see the caves from here?"

"No, are you kidding, centurion? Who could possibly do that?" He laughed aloud and then whispering, "I know we are immortal, but we still have the eyesight we once had."

"I don't, I can see them."

He backed up on his horse in astonishment, then his face calmed to understanding.

"It is our goal, you are determined to meet it, and so you can already see it. I can feel the presence of the spirit world, Thanos oversees the dead, Ardin conquers flame, and you already conquer your goal before it occurs. You must have this gift because you are our leader. All your gifts: mind ordering, sight, the angst you feel, they all drive you toward your purpose. You are a compass."

He returned to his former station at the back of the line after relaying this message. It seemed hard to take this in. Was I what I was given, or was I truly myself? Was not I only moments ago asking why I had no special power to myself in aggravation? I seemed a lost compass with this new knowledge given me by the most astute immortal I would ever know. His knowledge though, was it given him by this new life, or was it simply, who he was as well?

As we trekked in formation, my thoughts started to drive me mad. I shook off the feeling of insanity, and realized The Zohar would have no answers for this one. I had yet to read the mystical book written by the angel and given to the first of God's precious creation: the very book that brought dissension amongst the angels by this act. Why would they not want mankind to know about the beauteous mysteries of God? Was it He who gave me this power or was it simply the blood that created my afterlife, my nightmare, my purpose? All I knew was that I was not this way before and there were no answers. My curiosity may never be stifled and I continued to exist. My insanity was in vain. It was interrupted by a dark figure merging in the distance.

Gad yelled from behind "This was what I feared, Centurion! Do you feel it?" He raced forward and was now beside me again.

Eulogy

"No, Gad, but I see it. What is it?"

"More dark then the slain evil I came across, Centurion. Oh, it is an evil unlike I've ever felt before. My skin crawls with its presence. There is many, very many Centurion. I feel we may be doomed in our quest of the caves."

"*No,*" I whispered to myself and looked in their direction. I saw the one figure becoming larger along the horizon. "What should we do, Gad?"

"You are the centurion. My fear may be completely unwarranted."

"Why would you say such terrible things then to destroy my already failing confidence, Gad?"

I said this a little too loudly; the others looked at me in shock. Would I forever be an idiot? I could not keep up this mask for long. It was far too easy to be free with my speech in the vicinity of my astute conversationalist.

"I apologize, Gad. My feelings are far too open in front of you. Forgive me my, friend."

"There is nothing to forgive, we all falter now and again," he smiled at me. "How do we kill it?"

That was a good question. Gad could sense the evil, but not the vanquishing of it. Was it my job as centurion to know this? I laughed at myself for inwardly asking this.

"How should I know? I have never encountered wraiths or demons before as you have, Gad. I was hoping you would know."

This commotion stirred the others.

"What is going on?" Ardin asked.

Thanos looked at us curiously; Nen seemed unnerved and strode behind us. The others whispered chaotically amongst themselves.

I stopped and turned Marcellus around in front to address the others. In a stout voice, "LISTEN! We are about to be attacked. I want all in formation tightly around the scribes. All scribes, young and old in the wagon, *right now*!"

They obeyed without the assistance of a mind order. The formation was beautiful. I was proud of their alert obedience.

"Weapons at the ready! We will not charge. We will move toward our destination without their awareness of our knowledge. I want demeanor calm and prepared. We will not look shocked but we will be courageous when we meet them head on. UNDERSTOOD!?"

Eulogy

All raised weapons high with a Spartan yell 'HOU ... HOU!!' I turned Marcellus around, stature high, and backed him up inside the formation, nose ahead of Fatality and Brutus, raising my left fist beside my ear and vertical, then high above my head to move the line. Centurion strength within me, all inept ability vanishing on my face and hiding with in me- deeply seeded in fear.

The dark form in the distance waved into clarity. I spied two dragons under a beautiful black winged angel- one black, one gold. Along the line, odd creatures walked beside them. A great giant, bare chest with a lion's head rode a pale light-green horse on the left. Another great giant beside him walked, twitching a monkey's tail. A dwarf-like middle-aged man, with curls protruding from all pores of his head wore a great golden crown and rode a red steed. Another red dragon rider, with dark sienna skin, goat horns, hooves and a forked tail rode beside the middle-aged man. An immense stork, eight feet tall, strolled pigeon-like on his right. Another pale rider, wearing a silver crown of emerald jewels rode beside the stork. On the far left, strode a great black wolf bearing large leather griffon-like wings.

All manner of vile and enormous parasites, arachnids, and unseen beasts formed behind the line. They were beasts only written about in our myths; the same myths that Gabriel said were created to explain our existence. In that moment, I greatly regretted not changing Gad's steed, if it were possible. Some powers remained limited to our unity. I swallowed hard as the space between us diminished.

The horizon's line horrified into reality for the mortals: their faces did not obey the prior order I gave them. We attempted to shield this from the opposition's sight. The whole of them laughed darkly at us. The black winged angel raised his fist in the same manner as I to order the charge and opened his mouth to speak.

In succession from left to right: blue, white, scarlet, gold, and violet flashed before us. The charge was interrupted. The adversaries' eyes were wide as plates. The flashes solidified into five ethereal beings.

The blue flash formed into a sapphire dragon with amethyst eyes ridden by an angel clothed

Eulogy

entirely in white. He held a ten foot staff, yielding a blue pennant bordered with white. Two eyes placed on the left and right top corner within the blue of the flag. Underneath the eyes, two white lightning flashes on either side a gold sickle stood with in the blue also. The blade of the sickle was turned upward the staff diagonally stood to the left.

The angel looked childlike in comparison to the dragon and the other beings. His hair was cropped short and shimmered golden blond. His eyes were bright light blue and grey. The feathers glistening, draping his wings, the same sapphire as the dragon he mounted.

Gabriel formed beside him, more other worldly than I had ever seen him when he came to me before. He wore an azure sash over his white robe and bore the gold scythe depicted on the flag. White glowed around him as the aura of a mortal.

In the middle and at the head of the formation, stood a warrior- like angel, taller than the others by an entire head. He wore a carnelian cape attached to a bronze breast plate. A royal blue tunic shown underneath the armor and a Venetian red sash wrapped over top from right shoulder to left waist.

A.R. Perkins

His leather sandals strapped upward to his knees. His hair was medium auburn and shoulder length. His eyes a darkest maple tree bark color. His weapon, from waist to heel, was a broad edged sword. The fuller was the width of his two enormous arms. The grip made entirely gold, the length of three palms. The pommel: two ten inch golden wings. The point was diamond sharp. I was in awe of that sword. If only I could have this weapon, I would never fear another dark and evil thing again.

The golden flash embodied an angel, not too different from the flash that brought him. Our eyes still strained at the sight of him, as though we were looking at the sun itself. After a bit of staring, my eyes adjusted beyond the bright glow he emitted. The first thing I noticed was the robe he wore from waist to heel was consumed entirely of flames. Each tongue flickered from orange to yellow as the breeze blew them into motion. His feet were covered by this attire, as he floated on a broad and wide disk of glass. This star like shirtless being bore a bronze tone, amber eyes, and bright golden short hair. The locks never stayed in place on his

Eulogy

brow, but moved as the flickering flames in his tunic did, high above his head. His hands before his abdomen held a floating orb of brilliant yellow fire. The weapon shone its own aura and circled within and all about itself- colors changing light to darker yellow, ever changing to orange or red as his robe did.

The final flash of violet formed a man-like angel. If not for his Byzantium wings, he would have looked completely human. He bore an apothecary cap, purple velour pantaloons and vest, a white shirt underneath with frills at the sleeves, and a red suede bag strapped to his hip by uncommon golden thread. His dress was a site, and I fought myself with laughter. Compared to the others, I wondered of his purpose in this line of unreal beings.

After taking in the site, I noticed, the space between the adversary and the newly acquired soldiers had greatly receded. The evil ones were shocked, but unafraid of the relief we suddenly obtained. Only fifty feet, give or take separated the ethereal beings from our tiny band, and five to seven yards separated the evil ones from them. The middle warrior-like angel spoke first, "I will go negotiate with them."

"Be careful, Michael," Gabriel said, "We will be at the ready for you if we are needed."

Michael nodded his head and sauntered like water toward the line. The dark angel-like man nudged his dragons toward Michael in the middle of the desert. Michael must have asked him in a lower voice inaudible to us, for when he answered he pointed at Gad and yelled ferociously.

"Your angel killed my Chimirias!"

Gabriel spoke with condescending amazement in his direction unafraid, "So you bring with you all the royalty of the legions of Hell and your own creation to take out your vengeance? Could Marbus not heal your Chimiras, Belial?"

Enraged, he retorted, "That is not the point. He . . ." pointing again at Gad.

Michael cut him off, "He is one of us. This war started long ago when you fell from your seat and tricked Yahweh's creation into your vile plan. The dark rider threatened our sacred scriptures and their writers. Ironically it seems you bring this army of yours as they cross the desert, instead of coming

Eulogy

after our servant when he is alone."

Belial snapped, "*Regardless*, he *will* pay for this! I do not care if we have to destroy *all* of you! After my dragons have fed on his flesh, I will take the scribes and their creation for myself. The words will not be read nor continue to be written. The Son of God's works will be undone. Every soul will belong to *me*!"

Michael smiled at this, "Ah, yes," he looked down and chuckled. "The greatest power that Satan has is telling man that he does not exist. There is no evil without good, if no peace then only war: that is all any of you ever know."

Michael's epiphany determined Belial's destructive quest all the more. He raged thunder within his throat, his eyes burning red with rage, the veins protruding from his biceps and brow, motioned on the first wave of attack. The great buzzards and ravens flew onward at Michael. Minotaur and aerotaurum charged their great spearing horns. Giant spiders and scorpions crept with many limbed speed. If my heart could beat right now, it would have stopped. The elders were shunned away in the cloaks of the younger scribes, for fear that theirs would.

Michael stepped softly backwards and raised his great sword. He cut through the air swiftly toward one Minotaur, tar spilt to the ground and two halves lay. Another aerotarum received the blow in the same swipe, he lay in pieces also. The flying creatures floated overhead, waiting to strike. To the side, three horned beast speared Michael from behind to the ground with their invisible speed.

"*Uriel!*" Michael yelled from beneath the hoard.

The scavengers descended. A golden liquid started to seep into the sand.

Uriel raised his orb and opened his hands to the length of his arms. The orb expanded the width of the desert war field. Then he forced his palms out and the stream pulsed forward across the entire dark band of attackers. The human-like angel and Gabriel ran forward to aid in Michael's escape. Uriel's attack singed the feathers of the scavengers, but only fazed them a little. This was long enough for Gabriel to scythe the others, decapitating some. The buzzards and ravens shook off the burnt remains, balding in spots. This attack only made them flightless, but their sharp beaks still pecked at

Eulogy

the flesh of Gabriel and the other angel. Gabriel swiped his scythe again; they hopped back away from the blows, enough for the man-like angel to gather Michael up. He retreated quickly to the caves.

"Don't forget this!" Gabriel grabbed up the sword and tossed it to him; the purple angel caught it with ease, swung it around to his side, and continued to flash into invisibility.

The flashing ethereal soldiers that had me in awe were taken by surprise by this hoard of evil. I became sorely disappointed and greatly in fear. Gabriel had been injured; Michael had been slaughtered, regardless of the immensity of his sword; the velour angel had been attacked as well. Uriel's attack with his amazing tiny star-like weapon did nothing but mar the first wave of attackers. Giant fleas, wasps, mosquitoes, and flies would be on us with the second attack in an instant, if the flaming band had not destroyed them and laid them to dust. I was grateful for this tiny blessing. We knew that fire would harm the flying demons, but the spiders and scorpions, upon a closer view were made of rock and molten lava. The Minotaur and aerotarum continued in their charge. Gabriel and the childlike dragon rider stayed. We stood in formation and braced for the onslaught.

Gabriel waved his scythe from left to right and about his head again and again, taking down several only around him and within the scythe's reach. The sapphire dragon swiped his great paw at the arachnids. The scorpions attempted to stab his scales and were unsuccessful. The beast snapped at the tails and removed them with his razor fanged powerful jaws. It protected the child at every angle, while the mounted aberrant fighter swung the staffed flag clumsily. The first wave had not yet finished their pursuit on us before Belial waved on the second attack.

These, I assumed were the lesser demons and wraiths. Black shadows rose from the ground of the other attackers and took on a life of their own. Malformed humans of tiny statures and many limbs crawled toward us. I wondered what the leader was thinking, holding off these unnatural and slow creatures for the second wave, until the shadows possessed them. They grew to ten times their former size and stood tall as the mountains we were

Eulogy

headed toward. Their bodies were horrid to look at. Their hideousness varied uniquely. Eyes, legs, and arms grew from their torsos. Some had many heads and tails of scorpions and lizards, scales erratically fitted in places, balding scalps, and contorted joints. Every step they took grew the fear within us, and there was still another wave of attack to go.

One giant hand swiped Gabriel to the ground. The remaining flying demons stayed overhead circling. The sapphire dragon retreated behind our line. The boy's loyalty was to Gabriel, not to us. He ran over to Gabriel, yards away, and helped him up to the dragon. They all retreated to the caves. It was us now.

Aristos motioned to his fraternal twin brother Atalo in the direction of the wagon. They ran to it, one on each side, removed the horses swiftly and dragged the wagon, full force to the caves.

I was impressed with the initiative until Ardin chimed up, "I ordered Aristos to take the scribes to safety."

With this knowledge, the soldier seemed to read my instruction without vocalizing it. We all flashed into a protective formation as the brothers did this.

A.R. Perkins

We did not consider the consequences of exposure in our speed. It was I at the front center, Ardin at the right, Thanos at the left, Nen, Gad to the right of Ardin. All the newly transitioned were strangers to me. I had to be introduced.

After Ardin settled into his rightful place with Brutus he took that liberty and described the others, "That is Therius and Eryx standing to the left of Thanos. Bedros and Nuri are standing behind Nen and Gad, Jairus is standing behind Eryx."

He then spoke a bit more quietly, "While you were gone, as you know many were changed vehemently. Most did not take it well at all, but Aristos and Atalo showed great strength and even help me restrain Marcus. No explanation was needed for them to accept this life. We bonded quite a bit in the weapon room and we discovered they share my gifts."

I nodded to him, Adam's apple in my throat. The legion of Hell advancing, all this conversation seemed only a flit of time.

"Time to shine, Militia," This was another mind order, partly for me because no matter how much training and experience I had, the instincts of war

Eulogy

had never encountered anything like this.

Just then, as the malformed giants shook the earth with their stomping charge and raised their hands to strike, Jairus and Nuri did just that- from their palms and all about us formed a wide band of white light. It grew exponentially taller and wider spanning the whole of the plain. The giants' hands swiped down at us inside it and were completely stationed in their pose. Their many eyes turned to us, then to each other. They attempted to move, unsuccessfully.

Thanos stirred Fatality to charge from the far left of the field with his sharp sickle. He swiped through the limbs holding the grotesque beings up. Jairus and Nuri released their shield and they fell to the ground, limbs writhing in a life of their own. Thanos smiled at himself proudly and nodded another to Nuri and Jairus. Pride definitely goes before the fall. A buzzard swooped a kamikaze dive once the shield had been released- tumbling us over with his massive wingspan. One after another, they all followed suit. Jairus and Nuri forced themselves crawling to the back of the gusts and let their light shine again. Their shields stopped them midflight.   Before we had awakened from the commotion, the giants' limbs had become beings of their own. There were four times as many now then prior-the new limb creatures smaller than the original attackers.

Ardin became exasperated with this. Utilizing the force that worked against the beings trapped in the shield, he grabbed his flail with both hands. His body started to turn red and his hands flame. He jolted the handle of the flail with his power and began to swing- in front of him, expanded the chain, growing the glow of the ball at the end, then above his head as Gabriel had before with his scythe. We ducked to the ground. Even Nuri and Jairus were in line sight of the frightening flame. They stopped their hold in the terror of the threatening thud against their skulls. They had held it though just long enough for the birds to be slain by the flail of fire.   One touch burnt all feathers of the four creatures. The blow crushed their bones to the ground. Their bodies blew into dust in the sand.

"Anybody wanta eat some crow!" Ardin yelled at Belial and his army, grimacing.

I whispered in his direction, eying him

Eulogy

concerned, *"Do you really think taunting him is a good idea, Ardin?!"*

He only smiled at me, and continued flailing high above all our heads. Nuri and Jairus held their position.

"We need our beasts. Merkabah," I shouted.

We needed to act and act quickly. Simultaneously as the steeds changed to dragons, Bedros, Eryx, and Therius found their niche as well. Bedros threw boulders that he called from the mountainside up into the air. Therius caught them midflight with gusts of wind and threw them at the giants. Eryx rushed over to the pinned enemies and crushed the boulders with his hands, beating them into submission. The molten arachnids also became rubble as he pummeled them. Each time the giants rose up, the attack would start over.

Fatality, Brutus, and Marcellus shone their precious stoned scales in the evening sun. Their wings flit toward the remaining flying demons and crushed their bodies on them to the ground. They clenched their jaws over the heads and ribs, turning them also to dust. The entire fleet of flying creatures was destroyed. The giants were an entirely different feat. They could not be sliced apart, nor crushed, nor beaten. I had their source of power and rejuvenation. The boulders and hands of stone kept them at bay, but we could not continue this until the end of days. There had to be something that could destroy them entirely.

Belial had yet another attack in the wake. He toyed with us confidently. All these creatures, only shells of the powers of Hell- their essence awaiting renewal in the depths, fueled by Sommeilian and aided by Verrinne. A man of flame emerged from the adversary's line, gliding a trail of glass and soot behind him. Tiny flames followed him in a line in front of the royalty of Hell. Then the royalty followed slowly to attack.

The adrenaline assisted my mind at their weakness. Nen and Gad had done little in this battle while the other's great powers were exposed.

"Gad! The wraiths possess the giants! Destroy them!"

He understood immediately. Once the giants were down for the unaccountable consecutive time, as the flaming demon and his tiny clones began the assault, as the insects became dust, the molten rock

Eulogy

arachnids: rubble, thanks to Eryx's hands of stone, after all this, I was the one that knew the weakness. I was the one who pursued the goal- the key to stop this incessant insanity.

The wraiths of smoke attacked Gad in the desert. Gabriel had given Gad the sword of Lightening so that he would not fear the evil again. Clouds are nothing more that liquid smoke. Lightening crashes through them, lighting the smoke up and throughout with its beauty, cutting through silk with a razor blade. Gad raised the sword and put forth his power within- all the grace, paranormal energy, other worldly sensitivities, flaming love, and hope. The fuller glowed brilliant light blue, the point was glowing white. Eryx allowed the giants to ascend. Gad indiscernibly leaped and bounded up each ankle, knee, elbow, shoulder, and floating to the sternums with the sword. Each giant was sliced neck to pelvis open before any of them could blink twice. Our eyes saw each movement fluidly, identifiably. The demons had no time at all to react, regardless of their other dimensional reflexes. The flaming horizon hesitated in the approach, just aware of what had

A.R. Perkins

happened.

This pause prolonged their attack and Gabriel flashed behind us. The child with the dragon flashed in front of us.

"NOW, CASSIEL!!!"

Cassiel stripped the flag off the staff. The pennant disappeared. Cassiel threw the staff to Nen. Cassiel patted the dragon and whispered in his ear. He nudged the mount in the sides with his heals and the beast moved

to the middle of the battlefield. The dragon blew steam on the span of the enemies' line. The flaming man and all his clones disappeared into grey smoke. Their indestructible shielding was no more. The demon royalty's and their mount's muscles showed through their armored skin- tar seeped also from the exposed cracks.

"Ardin, Centurion, pat each other's steed!" Gabriel yelled.

We did so and a large clang fell behind our line near the cave's entrance.

"NEN!" Gabriel shouted.

Nen took the staff and held above his head. He then plunged it into the ground. The earth shook,

Eulogy

looking upward; we were in awe by a large wave ascending above us. Nen had conjured all the water remaining in the Dead Sea. It flowed underfoot of the demon hoard. Gabriel and Gad took their weapons and touched it to the ground. The dark ones were stunned by the holy electric current. The stork's slender legs wobbled to the ground- their steeds' members uneasy as they were newborn fowls. I noticed, on the line, the black wolf had risen up into flight.

Ardin called Atalo and Aristos to man the cannons. Their hands of stone were unharmed by the giant balls of fire they loaded. The wick fed within, reversed and was ignited by the ammunition. We stood far over to the left side away from the blasts. Body parts flew everywhere as the hurled flames caught their targets. All the royalty blew to a bloody tar of soot and smoke.

Gabriel and Michael ran expeditiously at the black wolf. They jumped up caught his wings on either side. The wolf cried out as Michael broke the bones within the griffon-like folds.

"You're lucky I don't cut them off, unclean traitor!"

CCI

A.R. Perkins

They all fell to the sand dune with an impacted *thud*.

"I surrender to you. You know I never really enjoyed being a Throne. I want another chance. Do you think Yahweh will find a seat in His presence again if I joined you?" The wolf pleaded without success to Michael. The tree bark eyes turn charcoal and he wrenched at the wing. The wolf cried out in pain again.

Gabriel paused and stood up pensive, he held up his hand to Michael, "Stop, friend . . . perhaps he can assist in our cause."

"Oh, bless you, you are not as merciless as they say angel of the final horn blow."

"Do not *bless* me, Marchosias. *Your blessings are empty and conditional.*"

"Then whom should I bless with my powers, Gabriel?"

Gabriel nudged his chin in our direction.

"Anything, *anything to be in His presence again*: They mock me for my knowledge; they beat me for my prophetic gift!"

"You will not commune again with the fallen. I will entrap you in a room of power until the end of

Eulogy

days. You will fight for them, and aid them in whatever they ask of you."

"I agree."

Each wing was carried by each angel as Michael and Gabriel hoisted the animal in our direction. I, distracted by his looks only caught his name. Gabriel was repeating to me the same conversation he had with this 'Marchosias.' The name did not exactly role off the tongue. I thought again . . . Mar-ko-zi- as. The beast then disappeared.

"Where is he?" I looked up at the two angels in their eyes, unafraid.

Gabriel looked at me ruefully, "Were you not listening to me? He is in the knob less door in the orlop. Only you three can open it. I'm sure you can figure out how, or must I elaborate on that as well?" He rolled his lightening eyes at me. We walked side by side back to the army, who was yelling unsophisticatedly, as soldiers tend to do after a great victory. Gabriel walked to Cassiel's dragon and she opened her mouth. Gabriel lifted her tongue and called Nen over to him.

"Here, you will now lead these men and protect them as we did today, forever more, you are now charged with these scrolls." He handed him a blue dragon's egg. "This will hatch soon, and will have the same gift as its mother. Keep it protected, more so than even your own lives, for it will protect all of you. Your staff will direct the waters and yield it into spears. It will also destroy them with its blows."

There was a lever on the side of the staff, a pointed hook flipped out of it at the point.

"Moses' staff had to be modified slightly for this purpose," Gabriel smiled.

"Jairus and Atalo, you two should also stay behind. The cannons will remain. Hide them well until the time is needed. Jairus will use his shield to protect the scribes at the entrance of the caves, as Atalo and Nen attack the sons of darkness." The words came out of me without my knowledge of their existence; I was still in shock that we had won.

Those that remained followed the leaders back to my Jerusalem home. The counters of marble, the cabinets, the window frames, and the borders, all of

Eulogy

the protruding fixtures were covered in dust.

After the cleaning was accomplished, I ordered to all within to, "Go get some more supplies. We will recruit more now that the others have found their niche."

I needed some time to myself. Either I was still in shock or began to feel the crowd within the not now so mansion-like abode. What could I do to remove this feeling?

Our army was dwindling considerably, though I knew each had a job to do, I felt as though, I should have more soldiers to lead. This was a thought in passing, something Gabriel had suggested, but since one mission of great importance had been accomplished, I felt there had to be something else to do with my never rest.

Issachar was continuing his conversation with Matthias after he returned from his stealthy witness of the capture of John the beloved and Peter.

He frantically stood and paced, "We must inform the Centurion of this. He has been gone for quite some time. Surely he should be back at his Jerusalem estate by now. John and Peter have a purpose, as do all the disciples. They were witnessing to the people and they were captured. I heard this while at the market place. I raced to where the soldiers escorted them under cloak and silence."

Matthias responded, "Mary is my charge, Mary Magdalene is yours, but, I understand. It is better to protect the servant of God than the mother of God. Her purpose is past, while his is now beginning, at least here on earth."

"Take her to Gaul, Matthias, I will seek protection for Mary and relay the message to the centurion."

Issachar and Mary from the house of David walked across town to the first quarter. Running up to the marble stoop, he pounded on the mahogany door.

"They took them, they took John and Peter!" Issachar shouted as I answered it.

"Come in, Issachar. Mary should be safe, but keep watch over her here just in case. If they wanted to capture her, they would have done so

Eulogy

already. She cannot be guilty for giving birth to their 'magician.' Make yourselves at home. We will be gone for quite some time. Eryx and Aristos stay here with them."

Aristos had shown great strength before and during the battle, so I left him in charge. His burly stature, and his massive dark head, would not be messed with, and with Eryx's capability, Mary would find solace here. Issachar followed very willingly as long as he had a nice place to stay. Each of them would have their own room, and we had already stocked up the cabinets, with non-perishables. Issachar had brought his great money sack with him, and I ordered him to pick up some vegetables and bread for Mary when the cabinets started to deplete.

"Let's go!"

This had been the third time they were captured. This time around, the Sanhedrin found a bi-law that would send them to Rome for riot instigation. The first time they were taken, the priests dared not try them, for the people were exclaiming of the miracle Peter had performed. He had healed a middle-aged man. The second time they were captured, Jophial released them both.

John had gone off on his own to preach when Issachar and Matthias took charge of the two Mary's. We had to get to Rome before they were executed. Their trial may be swift but they would hold him imprisoned for only a short while. We could port off the right side of Italy; the three of us would flash there at night and break him loose. Marcellus, Fatality, and Brutus, would fly separately so they would not die of fright. We would hide until morning and ride our steeds to the safety of the Galleon. The three of us had separate quarters far from the other guest rooms. I would have to bolt the doors of the other's rooms at night.

Oh, my! I had to be a stress sergeant now. I did not realize that the disciples were going to be such trouble. They were simple people until the fire got lit up in them. God had rescued them before, even with our angst and failed rescue attempts, He always seemed to come through before we could even become aware and flash there ourselves.

"Thanos, you must take extra care of Marcus, while the disciples are on board. We may have to put him in the door Gabriel was telling us about."

Eulogy

"That's an idea. I am glad the wooden awnings formed over the portholes. Marcus has to sit all the way at the end and the front bench to keep the sun off of him."

"I could really careless if he does burn to ash, as long as he doesn't do it in front of any mortals," I said, "but he is your charge, so you do as you will with him."

"I *have*, Centurion," he said with a glare.

So we arrived at the dock. Fedalis was grander than ever. It had been renovated for the followers of Jesus to be on board. All the same, old rooms were in the proper places, the figurehead had expanded prominently- two hallways, three quarters of great size on each side, a total of twelve. Judas was replaced by another man named Matthias. This was to complete the twelve that represented the tribes of Israel. This was no longer a galleon, but a yacht-like battle carrier. We would help them spread their message safely, without fear, for we would protect them. We loaded the stockade and pushed off from shore. The un-dead would have to row double-time.

"Eloi, Eloi, lama sabachathani?"   - Matthew 27: 46

Jettisoned

"Did you bring me the scrolls?"

"No, Emperor, my apologies, but their angels are too strong. They cannot . . ."

"SILENCE, you vial manurous fly feed, I made you ruler over the Northern Reaches for a reason. First your rein on earth was destroyed by the great deluge, and now you cannot even handle this simple retrieval. You are no better that a worthless DOG!"

"As I was going to say, most wicked and loathsome," for this was a compliment to the Fallen Angel, "they cannot defeat us if we change our tactics. We attacked them by land in the desert with legions that were born from the flame of Hell. Perhaps if we did the opposite, they would not use lightening, because then their ship would be destroyed. The fire that *one* is so gifted with could not penetrate the surface."

Lucifer looked at Belial pensively.

"Very well, see your legions to Marbus. We will attack by sea and they will lose their way in the Fountain of Youth. Then we will take the scrolls once the Chimarias has healed. We will take all proof that the Son of God ever existed. Attack them ALL!!!"

Peregrine alerted himself from his vigil of crashing waves. He stayed aboard his newly remodeled home, always in the wheelhouse; we fed him bi-weekly. At times, he roamed a bit and stretched his legs. It was not in him to attack as it was for when we were all reborn in death.

"To Rome, Peregrine!" I hollered to the helm.

"Aye, aye cap 'in," I only smiled at his salute; I ascended to his station and chatted a bit with him about the goings-on.

"Haven't they been captured before?" He scratched his head habitually, confused.

"Yes, but they have been saved before. This time, it's different. We still have to try, just like times before. I know Ardin and I were shocked to see there were two sets of empty chains after we had run through the four guards keeping them. Either, they," pointing upward, "don't have a lot of faith in us, or they want to test our handy work. If

Eulogy

Gabriel would have communicated with me that they were freed before-hand, no one would have been killed. Now, the story Peter tells of the rescue makes him look like a mad man."

"Well, I think they are all a bit zealous."

"They are supposed to be, but at least credibility would assist in their cause in spreading the word. I'm not even sure if we should be going, but we have to try."

"Why don't you just spread the word yourself? You have a witness too, centurion."

I laughed at this, "Yes, Peregrine, you are right, but my witness is for a very different type of Soldier of God. Besides, I knew Him for only six hours. They knew him for three years."

The men stayed busy reading entertaining themselves with other hobbies. Bedros, Therius, and Nuri played cards at the great dining table. Thanos kept to the orlop. Ardin practiced with his flail in the weapon room at the bilge of the ship. I took a seat on the figurehead's back and watched the waves crashing on the side of the boat. The sun was setting, and I watched its colors change in slow motion. The bright red orb fell ominously onto the water as if it would evaporate it dry. The clouds high above it transformed from grapefruit and deep ginger to azure and violet. The crimson splashed onto the clouds around the sun until it was gone. Then, all was indigo and cerulean. If only Marcus could view this. His curse was worse than my own. My golden haired beauty would have loved this site. I hated that sunset in that moment, too, she- always in my heart and my mind.

My feelings were interrupted by a sweet song.

"Oriana?" I whispered and looked around me. Only a siren could pull my heart as that song had. My longing moved my quickness to the side. I saw nothing but the waves.

"What is that?" Nuri looked up from his card game. Ardin could even hear it amidst the crashing he made. Thanos, who cared nothing about such aesthetics, even wondered up the stairs. The undead even wanted to follow him. He shooed the trail of wanderers back down. They groaned disappointed and descended. The men all went to look over board, entranced to the song. The music came from all sides of the boat. Each man pulled themselves magnetically to where they thought it was coming

Eulogy

from. The source remained hypnotic.

I felt a rush of wind whip above me and behind my back. My clothing and hair moved slightly. Looking up, I witnessed a great stag with leather wings, flying in circles above the ship. The others did not notice him, drawn still, as Narcissus to his own reflection, they were to this sound. Was I the only sane one here?!

Viewing my spying eye at his beast like frame above the moonraker, the stag made a large horn like noise, as an elk would. The sky turned completely devoid of light with in an instant. Thunderous lightening shook the vessel and precipitation poured moat-fulls from the clouds.

As they stood awed by the melody, they were taken aback by an elongated lion's head rising from water on the larboard side. The monstrosity hissed a great black forked tongue and bared jagged machetes at us, feet from their faces. The olive body dragged the underneath of the ship and wrapped its tail around the ship: dragging it across the sea.

Yards away, a maelstrom twirled to reveal a great giant. A tidal wave threatened to topple the vessel as the body rose from it. His melanin free body waist high out of the water, head nearly grazing the violent clouds. He raised his hands in the air and gathered the clouds in his palms. He, then, pushed them over the boat and pursed his lips to surround the vessel in the mist.

"All hands to the lazaret!" I yelled this but knew I had to be discreet.

The element of surprise would be the key. Our army dwindled substantially since Marcus pulled his coo. Ardin, Thanos, Gad, Bedros, Therius, and Nuri were the only ones left of the loyal. The rest had gone their separate ways to fulfill their purpose.

I whispered to Thanos, "See if you're undead can do anything to row us free from this monster."

I flashed upward to the helm.

"Peregrine, can you steer?"

"No cap' in. The gear is jammed up. There would be no way to fix it until after the beast leaves. This may be a ship of God, but this evil has a tight lock on it and it will not budge."

I flashed back down to the stable.

"We must go to the armory and attempt to be free of this beast."

CCXVIII

Eulogy

The followers will be murdered and these demons are conquering with that charge. My angst has consumed me now.

"We cannot wait long, but it must be a full-fledged attack, with no restraint. Slice the lizard to bits!"

Thanos shocked, "What will we do then!? We cannot wait here and let them take us where they will. Our mission is naught."

The nuisance's tail tip lay on the top of the stern. My spear was saved for only one purpose, amongst the demons, it would be too risky to use. That large one would use it as a tooth pick. The stag would grab it up in his antlers easily to give it to him.

The monster rumbled the ship as it spoke. "You can go now, Gaap, Vesper, and Rommel, I can take it from here." The giant nodded, the music ended as a green fin splashed away, and the stag evaporated into the clouds. Well then, only the cocky giant lizard to deal with.

Thanos look his scythe and hacked a piece away, the great lizard, growled a bit, but then the tail grew back instantaneously. Ardin took his flail, while the others shot arrows and javelins at the beast neck. They only bounced off and became wedged in the deck. The flame of Ardin's flail went out. Ardin grimaced at me in the eyes, "This is *terrible!*" He squinted while gripping the diamond handle, forcing his power back into the weapon. It blazed it again.

Peregrine's pallograph went haywire as the monstrosity spoke, "I am Forneus, the Duke of the Southern reaches of Hell. Pressure and fire cannot destroy me. I can swim through lava and devour corpses. Their onyx blood sustains me. My skin is asphalt and my teeth are diamonds. If not for Belial's order, I would destroy you all."

"Where are you taking us?" I asked.

The monster only laughed.

"*WHERE ARE YOU TAKING US, YOU VILE LEVIATHAN?!*"

"Where you will never grow old, many will seek and have sought this treasure; you will obtain it and dwell with in it for all time."

I opened my mouth to release my thoughts, and then recovered myself, we don't grow old! What was this crazy impervious salamander talking

Eulogy

about!? Even if they thought we were some kind of hybrid, wingless angels and not aware of the truth of our condition, angels were immortals as well. This made no sense, and I still didn't get a straight answer out of him.

We floated for miles, could see nothing through the fog.

"We should jump ship," Ardin said.

"What about our beasts and belongings?" Thanos interjected.

"Perhaps, that will be a venture for later on tonight. We could fly out of here, but not with all the others. We cannot see past this fog. Even if we could get past it, we could not get to the captured in time."

We gave up the fight and went about our business as usual, until such time as Forneus would release us. Months went by while Forneus stayed hold of the ship. After discussing our situation with Peregrine, he took the compass out of his binnacle. The compass spun like a top. To ascertain and seal the convexity, he looked at the dyogram and confirmed that we were completely vexed by this leviathan. There was no fixing this situation whatsoever and my chest sank into the bottomless depth of the ocean we were dragged through.

The fog had lifted ages ago. There was no land to see from horizon to horizon. We heard a whirling noise in the distance.

"What is that?" Nuri asked.

"Those who share your impending fate," the reptile enticed.

The whole ship shook with his roars and chides. We continued to look up in the sky for the noise. It grew louder and louder, then fainter as it went away. We could not pinpoint where the roaring was coming from.

We saw a stream of smoke rising upward into the horizon. The metal of the object it came from glared from the afternoon sun. We heard a faint long bellowing from its direction. The whirling started again as we floated onward. This time the roar was five times as loud. We saw what looked like black sharks with great wings. The points on their nose zoomed and there were men inside the

Eulogy

heads. We stared at them in awe. Five of them, menacingly hovered quickly towards us. Too close for comfort, we fell to our faces on the deck as they descended inches from the crow's nest. Then they ascended, into the cover of grey.

"How are you enjoying the trip?" The rumble started again below the ship.

"I can't take your mouth anymore, you overgrown snake," Nuri left to his quarters.

We all did the same.

"Suit yourself." Then he yelled, "You all were great entertainment while it lasted!"

We stayed in our quarters; thirst began to make us feel drowsy. We could not sleep, but our brains atrophied. Is this what dying felt like to the cursed? I dared not summon Gabriel after the battle that was waged before in the desert. Was this the time he would be silent? Was this what Hell was like without the presence of God? If we could not fulfill our purpose, then we could die, perhaps they felt we should die- our souls to never experience the beauteous freedom that the afterlife holds.

The end of time would never be. The Anti-Christ would never come, nor would he? It was I who had to kill the greater power of evil, and I who was overwhelmed with fear and incompetency. Why did I have to be the charge of protecting relics and martyrs? It was I who had the pleasure of slaying monsters. What kind of errand boy was I? Could God in His mighty power not do this Himself? This was the fate I wished for with all my being before when my Oriana died. I wish to live in Hades, to slay the Hydra, and float on a river of blood. There must have been those who listened to my prayers even before I believed, for they were being answered now.

Then again, now that I think on it, the demon would find a way, regardless of what we do or do not do. There had to be an order to things- a wonderful sequence of events. Surely, God would not allow His precious creations to be subject to the evil of the fallen.

I remember the battle in the desert and my thought retreated to Atalo, Jairus, and Nen. When I thought of them, I felt at peace. I felt confidence in their ability to protect. John the beloved, on the other hand, brought me the order of angst again. I could not see my goal across the ocean, so many

Eulogy

months away. He must be gone then. This realization greatly saddened me. How long would we be lost in this eternal rift of time? How could we return if we could?

Months turned into years as Forneous looped us around and around the ocean until he finally took us to the place he stated was the treasure men would seek. The second time we visited this place, we saw enormous metal ships. I wondered how they floated across the water, being made of steel and iron. The loud buzzing also returned in the clouds.

I had lost all track of time. This was the serpent's intention. I had to exercise my mind, the angst entirely consumed me, and I could not keep still. My lifeless nerves seemed on the edge of death. The ship came to a halt. Forneus left, being sure to instill the fear of escape in us beforehand, with his tormenting laughter. It was dark when I heard the sloshing of the waves hit the stern.

A shadow of trees lined the shore's horizon. I squinted to view a large campfire, the source of smoke rising through a clearing.

"We might as well explore our new surroundings." I jumped off the edge of the ship. I knew the men would want to stretch their legs and find a new reason for entertainment than their card games and lot casting. It was not as fun without something to bet on.

We sought the clearing. The natives of this foreign land were dark as the trees they resided with. They were dancing with weapons around this fire. Their clothes were brightly decorated with painted feathers. Loincloths covered waist to thy. The women, sitting in a circle around the fire, were the same, without coverings. Sticks inserted in their ears and noses were dangled with smooth black stones. Children, infants and toddlers, slept in their arms. All their auras were red. Great thirst consumed my cohorts. Even my mind ordering scarcely kept them at bay. I noticed a great temple. At the foot was a vat of blood.

We dared not interrupt them until the ceremony ceased. Many cultures would attack those that dared. The chief who sat on the pedestal at the head of the circle stood up and walk toward us. His dialect was an odd form of Spanish, but I understood him well enough to ask to visit the pool under the temple in privacy. He nodded. We drank

Eulogy

though it was cold and stale. Our minds re-awoke; our limbs were re-energized. The mothers woke their young-ones as the high chief started to share with us the legends of his people.

I interpreted for the others.

"These men remind me of the great leader of our tribe many years ago before the rains raged across the earth. Their skin is pale and hard as stone. They smell of the mountains. Their eyes are cold. These men are not though the same as Quetzalcoatl. Their purpose is different. They are not our god. Other gods are like our Quetzalcoatl, but they are their servants: cursed into immortality like the stars."

"They know," Bedros said, "we must kill them."

"NO!" I whispered. "We will take what is needed in time and as I say, but not now. We may be brethren with them for a while and we do not want to make them our enemy. Did the pool not satisfy you?"

"Their auras, they haunt me, centurion," Gad said. "There is much more history here we must hear."

I interpreted again where the chief left off.

A.R. Perkins

"Quetzalcoatl was one with two dragons and bore great black wings. For some time, he ruled on earth. He was in constant wages of war with all countries and pressed his will upon all of us. His army, winged as he was, would breed with the woman they found worthy. Their offspring would kill the mothers and tear apart their insides. Their size was great and abnormal. All their sons and daughters would help him wage these wars.

"Regardless of this turmoil, he taught us astronomy, foresight, the geometry of buildings, the origin of the earth, and asked for blood to keep our lands full of maze. We sacrificed our strongest warriors to him as he said he expected the best to be given. We continue this tradition today so Quetzalcoatl will continue to bestow his blessings upon us with plentiful crops and peace. We built great stone structures as we did in our former home, before the great rains destroyed it. We built them according to the stars, their rotation and the rotation of the universe. We have even discovered the end of time. We know when our own existence with perish. We have written these great prophesies down. We name our children according to the

Eulogy

calendar; we give them purposes in life according to their names. We abide in content existence here until such time passes. Many of us will be gone by that time."

This shook me in disbelief, I paused in my interpretation- I did not believe this. Caesars and mathematicians had the same quandaries about time. How were we to really even know what year we are in now? Does anybody truly know what day it is? Was the first human given the knowledge of keeping time? When was the starting point to the doomsday countdown, anyway?

The only despair I took in this was the knowledge that I would not see my beloved again. He stated many of them would be gone by that time. Many of these infants would live to be at least sixty, if they were careful in this vast forest, full of jaguars and poisonous frogs.

Gad nudged my elbow, "Welcome back, Interpreter." My thoughts drifted back to reality.

"Many years ago, before we settled here, we lived on a great island in the middle of that great water you crossed. Roads were built on all sides.

A.R. Perkins

All the great lands were connected to our great land. This is how Quetzalcoatl waged his wars using the fallen gods that bore giants for soldiers. Many were taken and made slaves to build and teach. The beloved were given riches and taught to adorn themselves in jewelry, as you see here on our women. We keep this tradition as well, for they are our beloved.

"Many have written of that great island. A blind man even gave it a name. Many will search for clues that it existed, when the clues lie before them here in our structures, and across the ocean in their structures. The Priests of Quetzalcoatl may have even escaped to the green land up north and built their mystical structures. I cannot be sure, for I have not crossed there, but my ancestors, the first to escape the great rains, have past these stories down. They may have even seen the structures himself.

"After the great rains caused by the vengeance of Huracan, four men and four women repopulate our world. The angry god lived in the windy mists above the waters. He spoke the word and land came up again from the seas. The first of us were Balam-Quitze, Jaguar Night, Naught, and Wind

Eulogy

Jaguar."

This story reminded me of the Epic of Gilgamesh: proof that if so many cultures told the same legend that there had to be some truth in it. After the toddlers had fallen asleep again and the topless mothers retreated to their caves, the chief raised his staggering figure and wished us all a good night. He turned his back to us and left slowly. No invitation was expected and I would have sternly declined regardless. This wise elder knew we were not human; he did not trust what we were not did he revere us as he did those he told the stories of. We would not be spoken of or written down or shared with other generations as long as we did not impact their culture. This I was absolutely positive.

Knowing this, I whispered to the lieutenants, "We have to go back to the ship and consult with Marchosias on how to get back," I said after the last story was told, to Thanos and Ardin.

"I don't want to go back on that ship," Thanos whined. "I've been on there long enough. All this hiding, I have finally trained myself to turn this ghastliness off in the dark. I have an opportunity to use it and now I have to go back to the ship, uh . . .

uh," he defiantly shook his head.

"Only the three of us can open that door, remember?!"

"Fine then, let me get my scythe, you get your spear, Ardin can get his flail."

We met at the orlop. The undead bowed to Thanos, slouching awkwardly. Eh, he heh: I uttered inwardly. I couldn't look at them. The hair stood up on my arms.

"Marcus? Where are you, Marcus? We have food for you when you are ready for it." Thanos yelled.

Marcus came from the shadow. The undead bothered him as well. What a terrible existence, but this was truly the safest place for him, out of the sun.

"Thank you, Lieutenant." Marcus saluted him respectfully. His eyes were dark red. I felt pitiful for the man. His thirst was much different from ours now- more difficult to contain.

"Let him get it now then if you want, Thanos. Bring it back here for him and let him roam a bit on deck."

"You know what Gabriel said. He is to stay

Eulogy

here with the un-dead."

I looked at him and frightened his glare into submission, "Gabriel, is a cruel soulless being that knows nothing about human life. He is the messenger of the end. This is only a chess game to him. *Let* the man stretch his legs a bit and sustain himself."

"Yes, Centurion." He became invisible and reappeared with the cup, before I could blink twice. I'd never seen Thanos move that swiftly.

"Now all you have to do is mind order him to stay on the boat," I solved the other inquiry, before it was asked.

"Did you know he can't see the auras anymore?"

"Well, perhaps he would be better served in the door here with Marchosias. I was not here when the slaughter occurred."

"I can take care of him, Centurion. He listens well enough."

"And, what of your creations, do they listen as well? I'm sorry, Thanos, but you should let them be at rest. It is not natural. Must Marcus be constantly reminded of his error, when he has already been punished by Gabriel so heinously?"

"I took their souls to their rightful passage. Are their vessels no more empty then our own? Who are you to order of what is natural: you with your murderous actions against me? Gabriel gave me this power and you created me so, with all the demise and darkness of my death. Now I embrace it. Now, I will do with this existence as I see fit."

I could have trumped this with my own power, but he made a valid point. Would it even have been effective if I tried? It would be of my own selfish manifests and not toward the common goal, regardless.

I chuckled a bit, "Come on, we need to get this unfortunate meeting over with."

The door at the end of the walkway bore a sun at the top with indentation within it. Ardin closed his eyes, glared at it intensely; he then, grunted loudly and swung the fiery flail into the sun. There were two long indentations for my spear and Thanos' scythe. The spear faced up diagonally to the right. I pierced my palm and covered the spear tip with the blood- then placed it gently inside the space.

Eulogy

The scythe turned down and to the left, the point to the ground, Thanos gripped the scythe tightly and combusted into the skeleton with flames for eyes. The scythe glowed in green flame. He waved the end of the blade at the handle into the space, then the handle, and the point placed forcibly within.

The border of the door glowed burgundy and the entrance opened when the door faded to nonexistence.

The wolf stood and stretched his wings.

"Where were you earlier when Forneus had come to jettison you from your mission?"

"How did you. . ." Ardin shocked.

"I know all things. Hell will surely miss me now that I am gone, but I will not lose this fight. Your side will win. They are harder to convince then you are."

"Well that makes sense, thank you for the encouragement," I replied.

"We need your help, Marchosias."

"Well," he smirked, "I thought you were just here to chat."

His laughter was a rumbling hiss.

"How do we get back to John the beloved?"

A.R. Perkins

"Ah . . . the martyrs. 'You must protect the martyrs.' Gabriel should have told you that this was an impossible task. To up hold your discretion, you would have to allow them to die. Do not fear though, for they will have their rewards- unlike you soulless men."

"You have not said anything to the others before you swore loyalty to us did you?" Marchosias was very intimidating by site and by virtue of his powerful mind.

"Were you not listening? I told you they are hard to convince. Why would I disclose anything to them when I am exasperated from their mocking? They see my sight as the once one-sided Omnipresence of God. What they don't know is that everything I see is based upon free will, but I know every way it could be before the choice is made. My mind is a giant calculator, tumbling through the infinite possibilities of foresight. Regardless, your side wins. There is one way that your side would not win. If I told you that though, the only thing left that makes you human would be lost."

"You said you would help us," Thanos said angrily glowing vapors.

Eulogy

"And I shall, but I will not take from you what you were created to enjoy. Let's just say, some things never change."

"Okay, thank you for the insightful background, but how do we get out of here?" I also started becoming impatient. The nervous feeling never ceased.

"There will be another great kingdom. This kingdom will shed light on times of darkness. A shadow will ascend and remove the peace and prosperity from this kingdom, crushing it to the ground.

"The dragons of Belial come to swallow up the greatness and to test the knights' virtue. The knights attempted to slay them and to capture them. Most were consumed and the dragons could not be restrained. The dragons will breed and head east where they are revered."

"What does this have to do with how we get back?" Ardin was getting irate.

"You asked, this is the way . . . fly."

"What about our ship?"

"Ask the Almighty for wings."

I felt so inept and discerned in that moment.

A.R. Perkins

Was I really so ignorant to think that Gabriel was the only one with vested interested in our purpose? I could not commune with God in the presence of this beast. His intentions maybe good, but I felt unnerved at his changed appearance. He was an angel. His choice completely transformed him into this ebony wolf, with leather wings, that spoke to us through yellow fangs.

I left, assisting Ardin and Thanos in sealing the door. Thanos ordered his zombies to sit still as they seethed at Marcus- hiding in his corner, ball and chain dragging behind him. Ardin went to Brutus and fed him raw meat and fish freshly caught. I sat in the fore cabin and prayed. I read The Zohar in its entirety. I prayed some more.

I went up to the deck; the angst in my gut was stronger than ever. I looked on the sides of the massive cruiser. I saw nothing. I looked everywhere, and sat on the figure head, my legs hanging over the wings.

The seagulls called. The waves crashed. The stress inched from my arms to my neck. I hadn't eaten in so long I could not remember. How long have we been gone?

Eulogy

"Where are they?" Issachar frustrated asked Mary. "I cannot protect everyone and I was charged to you.

I will not leave you but the word will be short spread if the demon hoard does not desist in this slaughter, there will be nothing left of the disciples."

Mary looked very solemn. "I knew who He was when the angel came to me. I knew he would die. It didn't get any easier seeing him on the cross, even knowing of prophesy. Now, all those that spread the light are shut into darkness."

She started to weep quiet tears.

"Shhhh shhh shh," Issachar sat beside her and held her, rocking as with a child. "It will be okay. They are now in a better place. God will find a way. Soon this will all be over, hope will be restored. Stay safe here with me."

"Poor Steven that wicked Pharisee, Saul, how could he do such a thing to him?" Mary wondered angry and confused.

A.R. Perkins

"I forgot to tell you Mary, Saul was traveling to Damascus and saw a vision of your son in the sky. He is now a changed man. He writes letters to the churches across the known world in the old Quorum quarters about his love and keeping the faith. His words are protected because no one suspects him of being a follower of

Jesus."

Mary looked up at Issachar and smiled. "My son is wonderful. He can change any heart."

As I sat, the sun disappeared over the horizon. It was still light out afterwards. The sky was light amethyst and the moon was waning new. Only the brightest stars could be viewed.

Thanos and Ardin found me viewing in awe.

"I've never seen the sky like this before. I just assumed it was there. I see it as a child sees anything."

Ardin said. "It is rather amazing isn't it? Do you think our souls are there, in that infinite mass somewhere?"

Eulogy

"I do," looking at him, I smiled. "As long as she is not suffering, I am content, but I wish I could share eternity with her."

Thanos, after changing, too comfortable in that state, said, "Even if you could go to her, where she is, you would not see her. The spirit world on a different sphere in time than our world is. There is no place, no time, no space, no air, nothing. It is void. It is everything."

"I would know she was there, though. I could feel her. It all just depends on what fills that void. Surely, our love could not disappear!"

The thought of that impossibility greatly disdained my features.

"No," Thanos explained, "the spirit world feels, remembers, thinks. These actions utilize energy. The spirit is energy, like the sun, or lightening. That is why, when one dies, the soul cannot run the body. Its purpose is no more. It must leave that shell to reside in its rightful place."

"How do you know all this, Thanos," Ardin wondered to him.

"It is my calling, to understand the interweaving of death. I am the reaper of souls."

A.R. Perkins

"Yeah, and you're grim about it," Ardin laughed loudly.

Thanos glared his flame again.

"Okay, you two."

"I have prayed and read the entirety of Ramael's book. I prayed again and again for a way out of here. My prayers have not been answered."

"Let go, let God. Sometimes, God will only help those who help themselves." Gad was standing behind us, eavesdropping. "We all need to commune with Him on this."

"How do you know this," I asked. "Am I the only one at a loss on this? How long have I been in my fore-cabin?"

"Quite some time, I don't know how long, because we do not keep track of time anymore," Thanos explained.

"The natives will know but their time is not calculated as ours is," Aristos suggested.

"They would know how long we've been here though," I said.

"Who cares how long we've been here!" Ardin's fists were curled. "All I care about is getting back. That irritating salamander and that

Eulogy

crazy wolf- how on earth are we supposed to 'fly!'?"

"To my fore cabin, Lieutenants!"

We descended and sat at the great solid table.

Ardin started off, "Well, that wolf thing said that the dragons flew to the east in his story. We have dragons, right?"

Thanos scoffed, "Okay, like our dragons are going to pull a yacht. Fatality doesn't even like lifting me."

"Well can't never did nothing, Thanos. Just because your lazy green toad of a dragon, doesn't like something, does not mean he can't do it."

His face started to flame to bone again. I was tired of his changing threats. Sure, he was scary looking, but I'm sure a bug was also just as scary when I first saw one as a child. I resorted to my skill.

"Listen! If we don't do something, we will be trapped here forever. Call your beasts, now!'"

Thanos put out his flame. They went downstairs to retrieve their animals.

The three magnificent creatures shone in the moonlight. This was going to be tricky, but amongst the natives, they were used to seeing many unnatural things.

"Gad, this was a long time coming. I apologize for the wait on this. Can you call Moonshine for me? We are going to need all the help we can get."

He did so, I, Gad and Ardin started the change first. The beast grew and she breathed out warm breath. The fur stayed without change. Thanos came last to pet the animal. The scales turned to pearl-ized armor, the wings turned to silvery foil. The claws even white as snow, the eyes abalone in their shades of color. She was positively gorgeous: more beautiful than all of our steeds put together.

"Let's see what you can do," I hollered up at her.

She looked at Gad and winked, then took a step back and away from all of us. Breathing a full breathe to her massive lungs, she opened her jaws. The flame emitted was a wide great streak of lightening. I felt true regret now more than ever for my procrastination. Her power could have slain all the water demons by striking the water, where the sword could not.

We rushed to the stable and retrieved the

Eulogy

harnesses. There were long tethers there also. All four of us returned and fastened the dragons in. We looped the tethers around the banisters two on the left and two on the right. When tethering, we began around the underbelly to shoulders, from there under the throat to snout, and around the other side. We had to work quickly before the sun rose in the sky.

"Go, Go GO!" I motivated flailing my hands.

Our hair whipped at the gusts, we habitually blinked rapidly. The jewels glistened- pearl, onyx, ruby, and emerald stone pushed upward. The galleon started to rise and floated along the surface.

Thanos shouted, "They're not going to make it!"

"What! Is that what your dragon said to you? Brutus says he's optimistic."

Gad affirmed, "No negativity, Fatality, Moonshine is willing to try."

"Marcellus is trying to lead them, but Fatality won't listen, mind your beast, Thanos!"

This attempt at controlling Thanos did nothing for his steed. That lazy animal: too weak for battle, too obstinate for assistance!

"Gabriel should have turned you into a mule,

A.R. Perkins

Fatality!" I shouted.

"Now you've done it!" Thanos pinched his nose and shook his head, looking solemnly downward.

Fatality raised his wings one more time and perched himself on the side he was tethered to. The whole ship rocked to that side, many of us hit to the deck scrambled for something to grab. The fire proof flooring was not the best for gripping. Marcellus tried his best to take up the slack. Moonshine and Marcellus drifted downward to match Marcellus' hold. They rested the ship back on the shore.

"Un-tether Fatality, Thanos!" I directed my order only at Fatality: "Merkabah!" The emerald started to turn pail as the beast diminution fell to the deck from his perch. I growled in frustration.

"Let us try again. Take your worthless animal to his stable keep."

The dragons sat on the deck panting. Thanos did this as we soothed and encourage our animals.

I looked out the side of the ship. The sun had already risen. The land that was once so distant in the east seemed so close, so clean through the

Eulogy

morning mist, for this was my destination; I was the atlas for the impossible journey of return.

"Now what are we going to do?" Ardin's emotions were my own.

"We will have to try again," I replied. Obstinacy was not going to deter us from our goal. I don't care was Marchosias said. The demon was used to not being believed, my trust for him was nil regardless of his talents.

"Moonshine needs to rest and it is day, I know we must try again but this is not the most opportune time, centurion." Gad discerned his reply. My angst drove me to lack of common sense. Ardin took the tether off of Brutus, hurled it to the deck side, and huffed away- mumbling something about females. Brutus glared out the side of his large red eyes in his direction, and then looked at Moonshine. His teeth glared at her. Moonshine's white scales turned rosy under her cheekbones. Dragons and their mental conversations: Brutus had made her blush. Noticing this, all anger passed and I chuckled internally.

"Alright Gad, take your beauty to the stable. Marcellus, wait here while I take care of Brutus, since it seems Ardin isn't up to it."

Marcellus nodded and rested his great head upon his clawed paws. The two descended with us drawn by their leashes as enormous pups. The stable had grown to half the size of the ship since the last remodel. Gabriel must realize that dragons need room to stretch their wings and walk a bit. They would do us no good cooped up and disobedient: a bored dragon is a bad dragon.

Gad and Ardin had an exurbanite amount of fish from their hobby by the ship's way-side. The thermal chest was stored inside the stow-away hatch at the corner of the stable. Gad started feeding Moonshine as I ascended to the deck to bring down Marcellus.

'After Moonshine eats, Brutus wants to be alone with her.'

'What like a date: How sweet!' I thought to him.

'Sort of like that.'

"*Well, at least someone is expanding on their love life around here.*"

I thought that one out loud by mistake. How could I feel resentment for an animal?

Eulogy

We had to get out of here; I had to keep our mission under wraps. I thought of what could happen if we did not fulfill our mission, of what would happen to my soul. Where were our second chances? So many questions riddled my brain. I was a map, not a fortune teller.

'Well then, you can stay up here and fly around a bit as long as you stay away from the east and the land. Stay high and to the south.'

'Yes, my master, I will return. I may even be able to hunt a bit.'

'I will expect you by sunset at the latest, Marcellus. We will try this again.'

He nodded and took to flight. I admired his stamina, though they had been caged up for quite some time. It was hard to trust them, even as creations from our own power. They were massive beasts and could easily get out of control, besides their appearance causing frantic hysterics in public. It was difficult to know when they should be changed and when they should remain in steed form. It seemed almost like a punishment to change them from their mystical form. We could not communicate with them as steeds for their mental power was not strong enough. Our new bodies weighed much more: the new blood within us thick with potency, our stone quartz-smelling skin and our cement bones, built for battle. All these aspects made the dragons perfect mounts for us, but not so perfect were they to eyes of the ignorant. In these times, and even in times to come, they would have to remain a myth.

Until the sun set, the boredom consumed me again. I longed to fast forward time to when I could slay the evil haunting this indecision. I wanted to destroy them all, to live in a time of peace. My existence was contingent on this ongoing war. Forever indebted to the hate I felt so long ago for the Son of God. Now, I should be punished with cruelty for my negligence that I practice here and now. The echo repeating in my mind: there will be a time when I will be absent from your presence.

I missed Gabriel's blinding flash before me. Before, all I had to do was think it and he would be there. I hated him, though I had grown accustomed to his necessary information. He gave me a demon to speak with instead. Now, I realized where I

Eulogy

stood in the scheme of things.

Marchosias spoke in riddles, where Gabriel was plan and to the point. He was doing this to frustrate me, to punish me. He stated that my loyalty and compassion for human life was the reason I was chosen for this. That had to be a lie! Now, I was beginning to become bitter, sickened at the irony of it all: awakened to my true purpose. These feeling of angst were brought about because of my own personality traits, not because Gabriel gave it to me. The map-like vision was a power he had given, yes, but maliciously introduce because of his use of said traits. How could those good, admirable, respectful idiosyncrasies be flipped into a flaw? He could do whatever he wanted to in pursuit of the prize. I was barely a knight; I was a pawn as well, just like Oriana.

Down time was bad. I mulled and stewed and burned with rage about this revelation. I am no saint, no disciple; I was in the wrong place at the wrong time. Oriana was in the wrong place at the wrong time: o, if only she would have listened to me!

That is the first place I am going to go when we

get back. Her timeless face will bring me peace, a contentment that will wash all the evil away. I hear nothing inside my mind as Gad does, nor do I feel the presence of out-worldly entities. My faith is what is seen and experienced.

I knew Oriana existed in my mind. I know she exists now with Pax at her village clearing: forever young. I feel the wind blow; I know it's real though I cannot see it. With all the oddities I have seen, my mind and heart- where it once was- felt only uncertainty. I fear, I regret, I question, and I exist in a place not my own. My soul lay dormant without these feelings. I am lost without the only reason for this body to move, to habitually breath and blink.

"GABRIEL!" Every muscle in my quivering throat exerted.

"*Gabriel*?!" I screamed again and waited.

I fell to my knees, crushing stone colliding with the diamond deck; chips fell from the knobs while I pulled either side of my temples' hair.

Third times a charm, "GABRIEL, I AM CALLING YOU! COME NOW! RIGHT NOW, GABRIEL!"

CCLII

Eulogy

Nothing . . .

"And it came to pass when the children of men had multiplied that in those days were born unto them beautiful and comely daughters. And the angels, the children of the heaven, saw and lusted after them. Then sware they all together and bound themselves by mutual imprecations upon it. And they were in all two hundred; who descended in the days of Jared on the summit of Mount Hermon."

- Book of Enoch 6: 1, 5 & 6

Emergence

I had to get up. The sun was setting and Marcellus had returned to see my distress. He heard me miles from there. Surely the distraction would have alerted the natives as well.

'*I'm fine Marcellus. I hoped my voice would reach the heavens. You ready to get going?*'

His head rose from my cheek and he nodded.

"Tether them up again!"

Gad and Ardin obeyed, retrieving their animals from the stable. Ardin tethered Brutus to the port side. I tethered Marcellus to the starboard side. Gad wrapped the tether for Moonshine around the figure head.

The three of us nodded to them and they started their ascent. We backed up against the wheelhouse to even out the weight. The nose of the galleon rose in the air, the sides rose as well, but the rudder grazed the beach line. The vessel dragged and slowed.

"Here we go again," Ardin bowed and shook his head.

"You too, pull harder, Moonshine ease up a bit. Order them Gad and Ardin."

The dragons did as commanded, the boat evened out, but merely floated feet above the land. My site cleared a different path as a crevice descent full of sharp rocks tore the vessel apart in my mind's eye. Before I could speak, Marcellus saw my vision and spoke with the other two to pull up.

'Moonshine is weakening, we gave her the light end, but the fall will push all the weight on top of her.'

"Help her please!" Gad and Ardin yelled empathically and simultaneously.

From the western setting sun, two fireballs flew above and toward our direction infinitely fast.

"Put it down!" I ordered.

The front end crashed hard as the two side beasts attempted to ease it down, holding her lacking weight. We stared off into the distance of the flames' decent and braced ourselves for impact. I feared the worst. The demons must have returned with the flame of the sun to destroy us completely.

I embraced an existence of emptiness now. I

Eulogy

had become used to the hole in my body being without me. What difference would that make now? I would have never thought such things before the loss of my soul mate, my heart, my love, my life, my faith, my valor.

I opened my eyes. The flames slowed and floated above us. They looked down at our shivering stances. My surprise was a very different feeling from the others- they relieved, I disappointed.

The flaming orbs uncurled themselves: firstly into a head, then wings stretching high above their heads, out behind to a furled tail, and then down to sharply clawed feet.

"I am Blaze and this is Nova."

The bright lemon one nodded as the tangerine one spoke. Their eyes glazed like rubies, Uriel's garbs blew nothing next to the radiance their feathers did as they lashed in the wind.

"We heard your call as we finished feeding the sun."

"How did you hear us?" I asked.

"Not you silly human, Moonshine and Brutus," Blaze nodded his head in their directions. Their bond draws us to hear their pleas.

I huffed internally. Marcellus looked at me cautioning.

"Don't scold me, Marcellus!"

'I'm not; these firebirds may be able to read your mind too. We communicate internally. I heard Moonshine and Brutus only ask for help after seeing the vision in my mind. They did not call Nova and Blaze.'

This power was beyond me. Is this power to ask for assistance only limited to the beast of the earth? Am I no longer at the top of the food chain? I supposed since I don't have a soul anymore that I am no better than an animal, yet these animals can commune with the caterers of the sun?

"We would be more than happy to take you back to the city whence you came. We will take the western road. We will have to make it back home soon and the sun will not set yet by such time. We will travel against the rotation of the world called Earth."

"How is this possible?" Ardin wondered

The crew looked at him and then at the perched blinding pheasants.

Eulogy

"We arrived from your star by traveling at the speed of light. Your vessel being made of the materials it is, at least in part, we may have to decelerate a bit."

"Our vessel: what about us?"

"O, yes. And you too."

Were all ethereal beings this cold? Phantom-like, they zipped to the back of the ship. Their claws in grown the tongues of flame; they gripped the banister of the bow, no singes of ash fell as I had expected. The speed was their concern, not the materials of our ship, as was mine. This seemed unreal and almost miraculous. These creatures were amazing; their glamour put our powers to shame.

"We have to hurry, Blaze," the lighter one intensified in shade with its impatience. The last glimmer slid over the horizon. Naturally they wanted to get home, but under the surface, I knew they did not want to be seen. Their brightness would be as an ill-zenith comet streaking across the night's sky.

As before, third times a charm; we started the journey yet again, even this excitement, which should have entertained me, annoyed me. The five spoke internally without reason for direction from us.

Thanos stumbled over his hooded robe from his typical safe hold the orlop, quicker than I'd ever seen him move before, "HE'S GONE! I TOLD YOU NOT TO LET HIM OFF HIS LEASH, CENTURION!"

"What are you fussing about?"

"Marcus, he has escaped!"

Ardin looked at him sternly, "Could you not mind order him to stay on the boat, angel of death?"

"I did, that part on my brain is constantly inside his head, reminding him of his heinous act against my un-dead, ordering him to stay."

"Did Gabriel's gift not work?" I asked.

"I can order the others but he has grown immune, or has been playing it off this whole time as though it had been working."

I sighed, and made one of the most hindsight decisions, "We have to go, Thanos. The aid of the stars has come to us. We have no choice and no time to waste on Marcus. He is better off here with the supply of fuel. Let him be."

"It's your funeral, centurion."

Eulogy

Another scene flashed inside my mind as we flitted through the sky. A man's voice echoed within my brain as I saw his nude broken body on a cross.

He said, "I saw you transform into the light of God, I spread your word across the nations of the earth, and led many of your men to their own death. Your will be done, your kingdom will come; earth and heaven are now one. I am Peter, the ROCK!"

I was stunned as I witnessed him give his last breath. Crucifixion was the natural discipline against those that would defy Rome. The unnatural decision made by Peter as to his position of unworthiness on the cross, brought his death swifter than the One he served.

Murderous acts and dismemberment were common practice in other countries. None were punished for their acts against the followers of the Galilean, only cheered. Truth, as Pilate said so pensively, the word rolled around in my mind. Was this the consequence for truth? Phillip was crucified in our absence in May of the forty-fourth year, Matthew was beheaded by a halberd in the sixtieth year, and Mark was torn into pieces by two horses in front of an Alexandrian idol. One of the James' died by sword. I witnessed them all, a shameful reminder of my failure.

One blessing though was that Mary remained protected at our home and passed on in her sleep. Her protectors said she was smiling, eyes wide and arms extending out above her. When we returned home, we made a glass enclosure for her as well, and I made good on the promise I made to myself by revisiting Oriana.

Pax greeted us as always, "I am glad to see you. Now maybe you can explain why I can't sleep."

We laughed at Pax, and dropped off the coffin.

"Protect her as the other, Pax," Ardin said to him.

"Yes, with your very existence," I reiterated, "One more will come."

We rode off. Pax had successfully built a stone home, much like the one we had in Rome together. Oriana's body was truly at peace. I pushed back the thought that crept within of the remembrance of her

Eulogy

soul. My mission was black mailed by this memory branded inside my brain along with her autumn hair, oceanic eyes, and auburn skin. I would never release her from my beat-less heart or from my void of a soul. My blood may belong to Gabriel, but I am still hers forever. I was happy to see her, enchanting and never aging as ever.

In the distance, I saw the Roman prison. The key had been revealed again. My mind reverted back to the reason we had been salvaged by the flaming birds, as they returned to feed the sun.

After all chores were accomplished, I was finally able to ask the Matthias and Issachar to fill in the holes of our absence.

Matthias started, "Lucius Domitius Ahenobarbus was born on December 15th, in the thirty-seventh year: his mother was the representation of a ruthless snake. She used any means possible to obtain power, to rule the world. She was nothing; her only power came to her by one more domineering than even she: her son. Her ruthless ambition bled through his veins. Her violence emitted in his actions, even as a child. His rise to power started while his uncle, Caligula, began to rein at age of twenty-five He was second in line to be crowned emperor. Lucious was no longer Lucious, his uncle and step-father, renamed him Nero at his adoption."

Issachar continued, "Claudius sorely underestimated the vial of poison that Agrippina was capable of. Regardless of his hospitality to her, she murdered him. This was only one example of the transgressions that brought the rise of Nero. The murders included Caligula, his wife, and infant daughter. At sixteen, he became emperor, quite a young age for such a 'man' as he was proclaimed such two years prior in the fifty-first year. As before, Agrippina, greatly pleased with herself, planned to influence Nero to her own purpose."

Matthias added, "It was three years until Agrippina finally made her mistake. Politics is such an insane thing.

Nero loved receiving support from his neighbors, especially after he had enslaved them. The Armenians had come to bare him gifts of peace and

Eulogy

alliance when Agrippina attempted to take the seat of Empress beside her son. The council members stopped her, as his step sister and incestuous wife was the more appropriate. Agrippina, repulsed by her son's infatuation with the slave Octavia Acte, scolded her son for his adultery against his sister. Personal friends stepped in to awaken Nero to Agrippina's quest of power and convinced him that she did not feel love for him unconditionally. He was finally able to see his mother for who she truly was. He awoke to the realization of the truth: she cared nothing for his happiness and only for the purity of the blood behind the empire."

Issachar finished, "Agrippina own spies overheard the conversation, and she divulged another plan in order to fulfill her obsession with the throne. She stated that Nero insulted his wife throughout Rome by having an affair. Agrippina defended Nero's wife by presenting her goal of blathering his indiscretion to the all of Rome to Nero. She threatened him with going to the Senate directly with the information. Nero exiled Agrippina and she roamed the desert. After Agrippina was executed during her exile, Nero was able to marry his true love Poppaea. He put his sister to death. Poppaea also passed tragically. Some believe Nero kicked her death pregnant and all!"

As they recalled the events of the last thirty years, I felt definite only a demon could do such things. Issachar and Matthias chimed on, almost interrupting each other of the slaughtering rampage while his paranoia thickened. Senators were threatened with execution; playwrights were exiled for their poetic license against any political party. Freedom of speech and the open door were shut indefinitely. Nero was emperor and no one would see to it otherwise as long as his power was supreme.

From that time on, the mental reoccurrences began. I knew when he slept, where he was at all times, what his intentions were, what he planned to do. All of this could have been avoided if we were not jettisoned on that boat. Gabriel could have stopped this though. He could have ceased these killings. Was Rome being punished for its own indecency?

Being educated in other cultures, I recall an old

Eulogy

Jewish story of a man who traveled to a town a stone's throw away. The Jew's God told his servant that he would destroy the land if he could not find five good people within it. The relation left with his two daughters and his wife had turned to a pillar of salt for looking at the site of God's destruction.

The daughters learned well from the culture they grew in. They became complacent to the rules that were set before them. They both had relations with their own father while he slept. Was there no morality left?

Rome deserved whatever fate it would be dealt with the ruler, this Nero that they so adamantly worshiped in his excessive expense, stage shows of murdering slaves, and the destruction of the only known word of the man left from He I had tortured and killed.

I saw no point to go to market but to find our own source of food. I was pulled to Rome like a magnet to metal. I became nauseous at the thought of the sea.

That night, I waited until the others were busying themselves with their own hobbies, and did something I dared not ever do. I took Marcellus and left to roam, as the dragon flies.

'Do you not want to at least take Ardin with you?'

"No, Marcellus, not this time. I wish very much to be alone. Thirty years on a sea vessel with that lot would be enough to drive anyone completely mad."

'Ok, just think to me where you want to go.'

I remembered the vision of the prison I had seen. Marcellus gained speed in the direction without another word. Marcellus could sense my sickening feeling as the sound of the waves strained my temples. The only sound was the waves crashing underneath us and the wings pushing the air, lifting us higher above the site of men. The stars above the cloud bank were a welcome site. The awing silence calmed me. This prison beckoned me and I knew not why.

Flying with Marcellus eased any tactful mulling I had been obsessed with for the past thirty years: the ageless awareness of angst never to be appeased, the ratification of rebellious revelry ever a reminder that we would never die, nor would we be at peace. Even if, I were to fulfill my vow, the

Eulogy

memories of this evil would ever haunt the vacant space for my soul. The enragement would ever exist in eternity with the enactor. I am mindful of my morbidity. My physicality of stone hides the fragility of glass within.

'Are you ok?'

"Fine, Marcellus, do not let me bring you down with my thoughts. It is who I am now. My sadness cannot be released outwardly. I suppose only you will truly understand my feelings, for I will not express them ever to anyone but myself."

'Dragons cannot feel as you do. I can sympathize, but never empathize, master.'

"Well said, my friend."

The bond I felt with this monstrous beast was stronger than any words could express: stronger even then my kin or my love, Oriana. No human could ever read my feelings or thoughts. The abnormality of our very lives bonded us as well. We could live without each other, but it would be as tearing the clothes of the man I had speared -cutting against the grain.

Marcellus dipped the leather blades of his wings, as he sliced the clouds into the night air.

A.R. Perkins

The mist wafted into vapor, his teeth brilliant in the moonlight as a grin exposed them. His amber eyes slanted towards me. Immortal children full of wisdom and truth, entertaining me in a lighthearted gesture, desperate for the attention of the act.

'Hold on!'

Marcellus continued to cut through the clouds, only they were above us and below us, as he twirled through the sky like a bullet. My nerves lightened from their heavy down trodden. I gripped on, knees and thighs tight against his ribs, forehead braced against his neck, elbows deep in his shoulder blades. I could not help but smile. Marcellus ascended from his plummet, head high, vertical, I raised my head as well, and shouted an exultation of glee. Now when anger mixed with regret and sorrow seemed the only emotions I had left, Marcellus became a sort escape from my thoughts of Oriana. The past thirty years were gone in that instant. My Marcellus had set me free, at least for a little while, from the stress of my purpose.

My heart may have ceased to beat in my chest and my soul may be void, but my mind is just a fragile as the day I was born. Break me to rubble

Eulogy

by pressure and you will find my core. Marcellus tempered the glass within me, for a brighter time. Oriana said I was her diamond in the vows we shared a life time ago, till death do us part. I am no diamond, no clay, no anchor, nor pedestal anymore: I am map and key; leader and murderer. I must relinquish what human I was and embrace this life: acceptance is vital to my mental survival. Would there be any bright days for me to shine? The answer to this was internal and the question itself rhetorical: not likely, only in this moment, in the dark mists of the shining moon, in the onyx scales glistening and the diamond whites of knife-like incisors. A form that would render any human to dust in fear, my dragon, which I loved, was not frightful, but whimsical and amazing. He would not be if not for my plight. I learned to no longer regret those choices simply because he was here with me.

After crossing the sea, Marcellus hovered just below the clouds, noting that humans were still about in the marketplace. The prison was only a few yards from the marketplace. Sleuthing skills were difficult with his size, but I had no heart to change him and stayed compelled to keep him as he was.

'I will gently land on the roof top.'

"Yes," I whispered, "stay here for me, Marcellus."

He nodded as he landed a clawed toe tip at a time. I dismounted Marcellus, crouched and peeked over the roof's cement enclosure for any bystanders that may witness my kills. My mode became speed and stealth. I flashed as if hunting a meal of hummingbirds, plucking their feathers midflight. I positioned myself behind the nearest guard on the far right. Before the final of six on the left looked to find the other five cold and dying, I had silenced his half unsheathed sword.

'Great job!'

I smiled wearily at myself as Marcellus had praised me.

'You stay down, silly!'

He tucked his head and slunk his back.

'Besides, you can see what going on from inside my head.'

I heard his thoughts of laughter and affirmation. He dared not laugh out loud; he would rubble the whole block. I cracked the sturdy, yet old wooded

Eulogy

door with a razor-like fingernail and measured up the adversaries. I saw several Roman soldiers, none of which I knew. Their garbs had changed slightly since I wore them last. A Roman soldier I was no more. Recruiting had ended since the jettison and comfort was a plus. I longed for that tunic right now; I could blend in and wait for an opportune moment. All these thoughts filled my head, and I was not certain why. Was I planning a theft? I might as well be wearing a black mask instead of a black hooded robe.

Many torturous devices decorated the room: the iron maiden, the rack, hot blazing red pokers stood in the corner by the fire pit. These just mentioned the few I could see through the centimeter of a crack I had created.

"Why won't you just die?" I heard a deep exasperated voice screaming amidst the crackling sounds of the fire and rolling thick liquid boiling. The sound was unlike the light sizzling of water, but sounded menacing and unearthly.

"I will only pass into the light if it be at the will of the Son. You may try to kill me, but your evil will not surpass the awesome power of the Light of the Word. It will spear your darkness and flood it for all eternity!"

Wow, who was this guy? I had to see. I courageously and cautiously opened the door further. I stood in awe of an old man, sunken holes where his eyes once sat, bathing comfortably in a cauldron of boiling oil! Regardless of my purpose, I truly believed that faith to such zealous was completely ridiculous, until I saw this man. This mortal man, who had been blinded, saw so clearly inside himself. He put faith upon the light, a light he could no longer see, but feel, and it protected his skin from the combustion surrounding him.

My spying was compromised.

"Is there someone there?"

The reluctant martyr's words alerted the guards and they immediately drew their swords and turned towards the door. I did not want to alert them of my unnatural gifts, for I could have taken them out as I did the other guards if I could. They had already seen me and a rapid disappearance would certainly raise suspicion to the demons within them. The tortured could not have known that his rescue attempt was so menial, only one protectors to take

Eulogy

him away.

The pack charged at me, and I instinctively drew my sword and charged as human-like as I could muster in my strain, hood flying behind me. In their abruptness, they knocked over the cauldron where the martyr bathed. He righted himself and wandered aimlessly, hands in front of him. He started towards the fire pit.

Regardless of his seeming immortality and the last thirty years of guilt encompassing my nerves, I shouted to him, "Turn around, FIRE!"

He did so and stood beside the cold red brick wall. The oil on the other hand had another course in mind. The geniuses that architected this and every major building in the metropolis of Rome skewed the ground sloping towards the door and adjacently to the grate under the fire pit. This may compensate for the leaky roof, but at this time sent my mind in panic. I had not been truly tested by fire: rocks, water, wind, demons of all sorts, but never have I been physically set on fire.

My mind blazed futuristic fears of molten lava replacing members of stone. What would happen to John and my reluctant army? The oil had ignited as the black sludge river flowed towards the cauldron. My thoughts raced as visualized reality raced towards me while the malicious wolves continued their human like pace.

The only hope I had in this situation was to fool them with my own talents. I grabbed up him and stood in the place I was before the soldiers could blink. They were a bit shocked and unawares at how the miraculous and blinded human found his way to my side. He felt me grasp and the speed had bruised him a bit.

"Sorry my friend, I will explain everything later."

He nodded and a tear trickled down from his crow's foot to his deep smile line. I could not put my finger on the reason for the show of emotion. I looked at it confused. The connections with emotion were lost with my inner sanctum in time.

The oil's next trek would be towards us. The soldiers were feet away and the motion seemed lifeless in my new sense of the passing seconds. I heard a crumbling above us. A whirlwind vibrated the ceiling. The soldiers' ears cringed at the sound of the scratching on concrete. A tremor quaked

Eulogy

outside. An enormous onyx forehead splintered the door to brackets behind us. Marcellus' high pitch screech emitted from his man-sized mouth. His diamond teeth were bared as he stunned the enemy into statuesque silence. I ran swiftly and carefully through the open space that was a door with the victim, holding his weight on my hip like a child.

"Marcellus, NO!"

It was too, late. The fury of the beast was too great. Emotions were immensely subdued for dragons; the release was usually exaggerated beyond repair.

Marcellus, seeing the key to the future in my head, believed that it was in its entirety, a reality. My fear had never been relayed to him in such as this manner before, and his protective instincts were jolted. The inferno's vehicle had turned the prison and all in it to ash.

Before daybreak, Marcellus frantically flew to the house. My new charge held on to me like a vice. If I were made of more malleable material, there would be nothing left of me.

'I'm so sorry master. I thought you were in great peril.'

A.R. Perkins

"It's fine Marcellus, this mind reading is rather vibrant. We must wake up the steeds. Rome is on fire!"

Without hesitation, buckets were collected from the barn and steeds were beasts at the word. They flew faster than light, while the three chaperones of Mary took on the new task of my rescue. The sea breeze had spread the flames. The clawed monstrosities filled their buckets as with the greatness of their hearts to put the whole of Rome before sunrise. The deed was finished and the flight to Jerusalem had begun, high above the cloud bank. The dragons again jeweled the sky.

A great voice yelled through the corridor halls of the palace.

"What happened to my Empire?"

"Your highness, a freak accident in the prison spread the fire across to the Circus Maximum. Many merchants are greatly upset. They want your head."

The short stature, broad-nosed man took his

Eulogy

small wide hand and gulped his throat under two digits. Thumb and fore-finger pulled on the double chin.

Nero hesitated and looked at his advisor.

"Well, sire, they have lost all their life saving and have no way to rebuild. They are upset about the 'frivolous' spending and threaten to riot."

"FRIVOLOUS?! My coliseum is not frivolous, its good sport. What else are slaves good for?" He laughed robustly in his nervousness and cleared his throat. "What kind of freak accident?"

"The cauldron of oil was knocked over and flowed into the fire pit."

"John!" he growled. "Those Christians . . . if not for him this would not have happened. Why didn't he just perish when he was tortured to the brink before?"

"Well, sire, the people want to blame someone. Why not divert the attention away from you onto a more convenient populous?"

"Hmmm . . . that is a fine plan, Seneca. Too bad my mother is not here to take the blame." He laughed again loudly in the presence of Seneca, but darkly   this   time.

CCLXXXI

A.R. Perkins

"Yes, Emperor, I will start the trials at once."

"I want interviews and no trial. Make them admit to the fire and punish them publically. I want their violence expunged.

The scene was appalling. After the "interviewing" process, Nero was pleased.

Hours became days, days turned into weeks. John remained with us. We fostered and protected him.

"Why do you not sleep or consume bread?"

A reasonable question and one I dreaded. I did not explain anything to him and I hoped I would not have to. His other senses surpassed his sight and surely we had kept him up with our stories and joking.

Ardin looked at me and answered, "We are the Army of God, John. We cannot sleep for we must take care of you and others like you."

John sighed. "Well, you haven't done a great job of it."

Eulogy

"We know," I answered, "Hell had other plans for us."

John started to cry.

Gad consoled him, "Now, now, you must be strong. God would not want us to be here if there was no future. He would have killed the centurion years ago."

John looked up, "I knew I remembered your voice. You are the centurion that speared Our Shepherd." He shuttered in fear. "You will not have that power over me!"

He got up and stumbled to the door. He was frantic. Thanos grabbed his arm, and he yelled and ducked his head.

"The angel of death!"

Gad tore his boney finger from John's fore arm. "Don't touch him!"

"He knows who we are."

I was shocked at this new development, "Are you telling me that you can kill simply by touch?"

"Not only that, but I can take the souls right out of man, and leave their bodies where they stand."

My eyes forgot to blink.

"I felt no such thing," John interjected, "it is not

your decision or power to take me to the Father."

"Well, then John," I tried to soothe, "we have something in common. We are both oddities with supernatural powers."

"I am no oddity, faith sustains me, and you are hollow and full of dust."

Gad spoke after a long silence of this pain. "True," we nodded at this, "but we have no power over you, nor you over us, so, let us help each other. Do not be afraid, we are both here to serve God."

FLASH!

I was not enthused, "What are you doing here?"

"Well, since apparently your secrecy is starting to fail, I thought I may have to step in on this one. Thanos cannot remain here anymore. Your vindictive act has punished you beyond repair. How dare you attempt to kill the brother of Christ!"

Gabriel took his golden reaping scythe and waved it in a circular motion. A warp whole cold and dark open before us. "This is Purgatory. This is where all un-dead will remain until you take them to their resting place. Notice the road is dirt and grey, this is where you will reign."

Thanos snapped his fingers and all un-dead

Eulogy

were there in my house! Fatality solidified before him. Thanos took this reigns and he never looked back for a goodbye.

Guilt washed over me like a flood. Look at what my selfishness created. My mind could not adjust to my sight. How was my existence better than destruction?

Gabriel had been speaking to me, but I heard him not. He placed his great palm on my shoulder and shared his lightening eyes with me again. I looked away, wishing never to see Oriana again in the state that he first showed me.

"Well, you've certainly made a mess of things."

"Gabriel, you are a horrid evil who knows nothing about how even a numb cursed empty jar of clay would feel. Why don't you just kill me? I release the spear onto Gad, or Ardin, anyone but me."

"I would gladly relinquish your power to someone more capable, but it is not my choice. Jesus sees something in you that I must be blind to, for it completely escapes me."

After Gabriel waved his scythe again to close the dimension to Purgatory John felt safer. He came over to me and grasped my face in both his hands. He looked at me as if he could see. Gabriel placed his hands on John's eyes. Light started to effervesce from underneath the angel's fingertips and throughout the martyr's sockets. A soft high singing came from the light. I looked at John; his bright grey eyes matched the shades in his hair and beard. I saw that he was whole again. My actions proved my over joy. I groped his shoulder and pulled him to me veraciously in embrace.

Gabriel defended, "I am no horrid evil, Centurion. I have learned the only way to motivate you is to punish you. You are faithless." He motioned to John, "This man, has already been through 'Hades' as you call it. You, brethren, have not. You now will, more so than you ever thought possible."

"Whoa, whoa, whoa, hang on now, Gabriel, how is this my fault because you felt the need to test me with your silence? We tried every means possible to chop that lizard into bits. We prayed and screamed for you. I read the 'sacred book.'"

"Where is your faith, Leader? Your own memory will not forsake you on your neglecting to

Eulogy

change Moonshine. The phoenixes were to stay on in the spaces provided you on the galleon. There is no room there now for the saints to stay on, and they are the most coveted of the demon's treasures. Why would I ask you to keep them on your ship, with all your murderous and blood thirsty soulless empty shells? The acts that caused their martyrdom was sprung upon them because of the fervor the fallen ignited."

"Then why did I feel the need to protect them so?"

Gabriel flashed away, leaving my question unanswered. His defense became vapor as I, of course came to the realization I had always presumed about him. It was part of his plan to obtain checkmate. He did not want the feelings I had toward him to be valid by his response. Furthermore, human nature glorified angels and saw them as the doers of the good will of God. The answer would have been given before John and that perception would have been void. It was easy for us to be the scapegoats of the master plan for we 'did not exist.'

And the Lord Commanded the man, "You are to eat from any tree in the garden, but you must not eat from the tree of knowledge of good and evil, for when you eat of it you will surely die." - Genesis 2:16, 17

Control

After complying internally with Gabriel's demands, I introduced the now vision repaired, John to Marcellus. He was the only unchanged human whose entire body, mind, and soul was completely protected from the attacks evil. This unnatural power was confirmed by Gad before the introduction was allowed.

John's mouth gaped open and seemed unable to verbalize the awe that stunned his new eyes. Still feeling helpless to the new quests to come, the feeling melted as John raised his hands up to the monster's snout. Marcellus lowered slowly and nuzzled them gently. They both shut their eyes in comfort.

Still saddled from the former trip amongst the commotion with Thanos, I hoisted John from above his hips into the saddle. He looked at me, wide-eyed in surprised at my strength. I promised to explain it all to him on the way to Patmos.

"I knew there had to be something special about you."

"*Special* is not the word for it, John."

'Away, Marcellus.'

We flew higher and higher, above the sun's shimmer again. John grazed his hands along the clouds as they evaporated into mists above Marcellus' wings. I turned to check on his status and saw his eyes squinted shut from the jewels' reflections.

I explained the story to him from beginning to end, he seemed more afraid of me then he was of Marcellus.

I turned to him again, looking to force reassurance, "You will be protected once you get to Patmos, I am certain of it. Gabriel would not allow any evil to find you there. My men stay with me, and the only other that may harm you, will not know your location."

He grunted affirmatively at this. I felt comfortable now that he seemed at ease with the prospects of his new home.

After understanding the miracle that I had become (at least miracle was his wording for it) he recognized the power behind the fluid that had changed me. He, in retrospect, commented on the way it affected him.

Eulogy

"The blood of Christ washes away all sin. That is why he was purged for our transgressions. By His wounds, we are healed."

He still did not completely understand. Perhaps he did not believe that anything could be completely predetermined.

The forks in life ended for me that day. The journey was set, though I traveled it blindly. "Yes, John, but in my case, it is incredibly literal. My soul is not healed; it is captured forever in the sword's grip that He will yield when He comes again. To repeat . . . I am *not* special. Only those who are covered by his sacrifice are the special ones. I will walk the earth until the end of time. I want nothing more than for it to end."

I felt as though he started to understand my plight, but he could never *truly* empathize. I could not expect him to. His life, though tested and purged, was full of peace and light. Mine was the absolute opposite.

I strained to acknowledge his ignorance of negativity that affected our presence on this earth. We murdered, true they were evil people, but 'there is no-one could not be saved.' We spread like a virus across all nations of the earth. Eventually, there would be nothing left to kill, and we would starve to death. We've even created death and monstrous fanged beasts that could not be seen by the mortal's eye, for fear of entrapment. I saw nothing good what-so-ever in us. How could the man I killed do so?

The isle was not far. All witnesses to the descent were far from sight. Marcellus landed and said his good-byes to the follower of God. He waited on the beach side as we traveled inland to venture for shelter. A cave was tucked in the mountainside, where freshwater flowed from the north. Fish played merrily. Banana and coconut palms branched feet from the mouth of the cave. Parchment and quills lay within on a stone table paired with a wooded chair. As I assumed, for once correctly, John would be well provided for.

Using my talents, I returned to Marcellus before John could remember I was ever there at all. I was hoping he would forget everything, and believe it to be a dream. Perhaps angels had brought him to the isle in the middle of the night as he slept. He may believe that *I* doing it wasn't far from the truth. I

Eulogy

scoffed at this internally, and Marcellus rumbled a bit as well at my thinking.

'Come on you, let's get home.'

I wondered about Thanos. My pull to him was always strong. He was the first I had ever changed. What if I needed him for something? His morbid expertise had come in handy, although frightening, on many occasions. I was, though, happy to be rid of his worthless steed.

Time eased by as we continued as we always did. We resided in the home in Jerusalem . . . waiting on my order. Eternity is mundane. Like packs of lions, once a week, we sent out hunting parties. We took care of Peregrine, as always. The ship was useless, but it was his home, not ours and vice-versa. He was not happy without the smell of the sea. It's amazing and huge appearance attracted passer-bys as it parked at the dock and Peregrine was constantly driving them away. He put up 'No Trespassing' signs and the dock masters took them down every morning. It kept him busy, though a great irritant to his habitual scrubbing and mast repairs.

After the update we received from the charges

of Mary, I knew Nero was evil. I just didn't truly understand his significance. Honestly, without the only feeling of angst or sorrow, I really didn't care. Boredom seemed natural now. It seemed a solace from my former life, so many decades ago.

With no humans about, we had no reason to buy real food or drink; no reason to act human at all. Ardin had contests with everyone to see who could blink first. He started with the dragons, then with the latest changelings. Eryx lasted the longest at three days, two hours, and forty minutes. From time to time, I would walk down to the market to buy a book or two. I could not stay there for too long, before the memories would start to flood in.

While in the marketplace, the rumors started again. Our unsocial habits made it difficult to hear them, but the time had flown by to us, while months crept by for the mortals. Ironically, the boredom became our entertainment, an escape from props.

One burly man whispered to his friend, "Word from Rome is, the followers of Christ have admitted to the fires in Rome."

"Yes! I heard that many were decapitated and displayed in the streets, while the rest were

Eulogy

inflamed to illuminate the night." Many were crucified; others were fed to dogs, and others were dismembered by horses.

The brutality of it all gave evidence that is not merely man behind the killings. This was nothing more than torturous acts against them to make them admit. Hundreds became human torches as retribution for the fire. They lit up the night along the road side to the palace. More heinously, starving dogs tore some apart and others were crucified.

Our over stretched vacation was obviously plotted to deter our quest. John was not among the dead. Perhaps he escaped! We would have to find him, for he would be vulnerable. Many things had happen while we were chasing geese in the middle of nowhere. My reason for existence had emerged.

Something must be brewing that I had to be prepared for. Why had I not been aware of these happenings before today? In came the stressed and useless feeling again. You know what? No! I'm not going to act! I will not be prepared for anything until my talent tells me to. My obstinacy surprised me.

Gabriel will let me know or I will learn of this by other means. I will not make the same mistake again. I am not a mind, I am a body that must be led where to go. It's not like any faith or prayers would help me now. What do I have to save, my soul or something?

I opened my mouth and laughed loudly, to the surprise of the other shoppers. I looked to the ground sheepishly, and walked home. I finished this journey after buying the <u>Iliad</u>. My curiosity about the Mayans' fable prompted this purchase. But what on earth was I supposed to do?

"We must act. Nero's had made himself a god not simply an emperor. We have no power left."

"My wife knew some of the Christians he ordered to be killed. They said that they hoped God would protect them from this evil, for many were tortured into admission of the fire. I know personally, that they all had alibis for that night. Yet, with a *swipe of his scepter*, he orders them all to die, without any trial or presentation of case

Eulogy

before us. He is out of control!"

"Piso, what do you think?"

The Roman statesman perked up his head from the chatter in the court, "The Praetorian Guard should assign a new emperor. To do that, Nero must go. I hear there is a centurion that has the guts to take this on. He has traveled abroad and knows several languages. He also has many years of experience in matters that others would not dare to perform. He resides in Jerusalem. I will pay him a visit and start on the matter."

"Just what is his name?"

"His name has been changed and his birth name has been lost in time."

The rest of the Senate was in awe of the power and the mystery of this centurion with no name. They mumbled impressed affirmations amongst themselves of the divulgence of Piso's plan. They were completely ignorant, though, to the true intentions behind Piso's devise. The head of Praetorian Guard was regularly bribed by Piso to perform his bidding. He would be emperor before Nero's blood fell to the ground.

Rome was beginning to come full circle. The

reversion familiarized of when the first murder began, when the first curse had banned the first people from paradise, when the Babylonians tried to reach the heavens, and when the first war was waged. Cities had fallen before, men had killed before, emperors had died before, and giants had been slain before: before this monumental moment, history had not changed. History had been written, the vicious cycle of history, would be written again.

I saw the entire meeting portraying in my mind. I felt like I was there. Gabriel must be rolling in the clouds of Heaven right now with laughter at me. He had given me an upgrade. It was like I was viewing a play when I was the main character. My mind the puppet and Gabriel the puppeteer. This state rendered me completely helpless. This was good though, ironically, as a soldier, I wasn't the sharpest needle in the hay. If it wasn't for my limited ability to stand guard at a gate, or for the purpose of provision for my Oriana, I would be a simple unidentifiable farmer. The realization of the images forcing my purpose awakened my self-worth: negative or positive. Still a bit conflicted and confused, I waited for him to knock on my

Eulogy

door.

It was night. An onslaught had arrived. The mansion of my home was crowded. There were too many to count and their names were difficult to remember. I knew that many were Senators, soldiers, and a few from the Praetorian Guard. Subrius Flavus and Sulpicius Asper sat with him on my luxurious white leather sectional, while the others looked for refreshment from the long trip. Another marketplace venture was in order.

While venturing involuntarily, we did not have the opportunity to spend our shared pot of wealth. Few vendors worked at night, fisherman and wineries, but the hoard of hunger had nearly dwindled our account to nothing. I never did understand how I was supposed to survive throughout eternity with little-to-no funds. My responsibilities made it difficult to hold a position of employment.

Piso spoke first, "We are in great need of your expertise, Centurion. These two beside me have assisted in devising a plan against the emperor, but we need your assistance in carrying it out. The deed is truly dangerous and Nero has spies everywhere. We have all taken a blood oath not to speak a word of this conspiracy to any soul other that those here."

I already completely understood what I had to do, it was what I was made for, and the question was, where would he be and could I get there fast enough. Ha! Of course I could. I could run across the sea if I so chose to.

My response was sly and methodical, "You may have taken a blood oath, but you must understand so have we. We are not just mysterious clan without origin with coveted expertise. If you want our assistance, you will have to join *our* covenant before we can agree to assist you."

The three seemed incredibly fearful of this. They did not know what we were and after my pitch, they had confirmed the appalled thoughts swimming before their arrival.

"All or nothing, Piso," I did not need them to follow through with the deed and there was no way they know more than what I knew. I needed an army and this was just the bunch to change. The ship would accommodate them splendidly. Gabriel did tell me to create an army and my army was a

Eulogy

tiny dent in what I would call a true legion. Their auras shown gold with indecisiveness. They were perfect. I fought my gleeful eyes and sculpted my face to stone.

"I will have to meet with them about this."

"It is already done."

We never had guests over without the special vineyard uncorked.

"You made your decision when you travelled here. What we are cannot be revealed for the evil you seek to destroy will acknowledge our existence."

Piso could not believe his ears. He felt different, he knew it was true.

"You will leave your mortal lives behind and follow me. Bring your steeds and hitch up your ship to the Fidelus."

They followed us to the ship and did as I instructed. The stable again expanded and the rooms had expanded again, wider and many more. The powers that be knew how to make the Senator's happy. The rooms were incredibly luxurious. The furniture within each room compared to the lushness in our office. The walls were no longer stucco white, but red lacquer with golden sporadic streaks shining through out. Their thirst would be insatiable; I planned for the hunting party tonight. Gratefully, the bolts remained on the outside of the cabin doors. There they would remain. The remainder of the originals kept watch on the ship. For now, the ship had a purpose again.

Nero had been taught the art of alchemy from his mother at a very early age. He believe in it powers, but had never tested them out for himself until the fear from the Senator's absence had left him at no other action. He had seen the magic with his own eyes. Agrippina had summoned all manner of beings that she confided in. They told her that her exile would be short lived, that her son would rule all of Rome, and how to accomplish the will she sought.

He knew the requirements needed to bring up the familiar he sought. The future, he needed the future. Did he even know who he truly was? How could he fear the future or the unknown?

CCCIV

Eulogy

Nero was rambling under his breath, "Everything is coming undone; I know it is. I can feel it in my gut, Epaphroditos. My mother did this," he then looked up and ceased in his rhetorical ranting, "do you remember the ritual?"

"No, sire, what are you talking about." The servant was greatly confused.

"Never mind, never mind, just get me chalk and candles and a book of summons."

"Yes, sire."

The servant hurried away and returned to assist Nero with the ritual. After preparing the alter and reading the Latin prose, a dark form started to solidify.

"Leave me, Epaphroditos!"

The servant happily ran from the presence of the obviously insane sociopath. The dark form became fewer vapors as he continued to repeat the verbiage. Over and over, he chanted the incantation.

"Ahhaaa! It worked, it worked, praise mommy, it worked: now, what to ask of this familiar . . ." again, having conversations with his self, rubbing his chin, and pacing about the pentagram. "The future, prophesy, what will happen to me and how can I stay safe from whatever Piso is planning? YES! Beast, answer me this, what is happening? Are my suspicions correct?"

The beast bowed before Nero, "Almighty one, you have returned, I will answer everything you ask. Currently, I am being held prisoner by the Seraphim that helped to banished you to the depths of Hell. The two broke my wings and placed me in a room only to be released by the cursed ones. They will aid in your demise.

"They have spread their plight to the conspirators and they are now like them, immortal and lethal to all the ethereal. You, Belial, are in danger of oppression again. Your disguise does not fool me, only you could reign supreme where others have failed."

Nero seemed surprised at this revelation and scared to death.

"Why do you fear the end, Belial? The one way that you could not fail to reign again is to commit the sin upon yourself. I failed to tell them this as I am attempting to infiltrate them. I hoped you would remember the old magic and summon me. I saw

CCCVI

Eulogy

this in prophesy, and you did not disappoint."

"I do not remember any of this! Just, how am I supposed to let it all end? I am happy in this life, sure there is the occasional rioter, but they are easily dealt with."

"O, yes and Lucifer is *elated* at the job you're doing with the martyrs. When he said 'kill them all,' you took him literally. *Wonderful, ha-ha-haaaaa!*" The beast evaporated back to his former state as the laughter echoed inside Nero's mind. The reluctant demon curled his fisting palms on his temples and pounded his forehead on his luxurious silk paisley red comforter over and over and over again, growling obscenities to the wind.

After the tantrum, Nero sat beside the bed, breathing to compose himself. Still completely confused at the revelation the bat winged wolf-like creature had shared with him; he finally just decided to give up on any kind of explanation. *Epaphroditos! Yes, he will know what to do. And Seneca, and my dear friend, yes, he will protect me.*

"*Epaphroditos!*"

"Yes, sire?"

"To the stables, quick now, hurry, get the maid

servant in here to pack my belongings. I must be ready for whatever may come. Just saddle the fastest horse be sure it is the most rested, and I will have to gather an army at Ostia, and . . ."

This vision faded as well. My thoughts reverted back to who I was. Had Oriana pegged me appropriately? In this moment, I remembered the semblances on the vase. My intuitiveness emphasized, I, the hunter of evil, now the proud raging lion burned by the very thing I mistrusted. Were these attributes truly my own in this life or was it the chess master again moving the pieces.

How ironic that Marchosias would betray me to hundreds of miles away and be trapped for my vengeance only feet from me. Thanos was gone. If he was the only other one to open it, *would* the magic work again? I opened my eyes to behold Ardin staring out the window, deep in thought: my only confidante, not animal.

"Ardin, *let's go!*" I motioned him. "Gather your flail."

We walked toward the ship. I walked sternly, with purpose, elongating powerful steps, arms swaying, fists curled, Ardin followed me oblivious.

Eulogy

I ignored all eyes on me as I trudged down the stairs.

I retrieved my spear from the office and continued down the second flight to the orlop. I inserted the spear and motioned to Ardin to thrust his flail. He did so and Death's Scythe appeared within the door, without Thanos' arrival. The power behind the scythe could transform beyond worlds, but at that moment, Thanos did not. He must have been wondering the purpose behind the disappearance.

In any case, the door was opened, and the beast shuddered before me. He saw this possibility in the abacus of his mind. He saw his own demise.

"You cannot kill me. The spear is lost until you leave this room, hence the beauty of the power behind the weapons used to open it."

He was ironically brave in his state of fear to speak in that manner to me in my state of fury. I took my centurion sword out of its sheath and slowly lowered it under his furry snout. I stared into his white-less eyes relentlessly.

"Ardin," I, still blink-less and intent, motioned to Ardin, "Marcellus."

A.R. Perkins

"He will not fit down here."

I looked away for that second to Ardin, "Not *now, he won't*. Breathe the word and get him down here as a steed."

The stage was set and the glorious black steed raced individually down to me, blowing flames from his snout, shining his garnet eyes at Marchosias.

"Merkabah!"

I watched the fright transfer slowly in Marchosias' eyes as the beast's reflection intensified. This pleased me greatly, all the while my blade upon his throat.

'Step aside!'

Marchosias was devoured in one gulp. He would never escape from the bellows of the brimstone within.

Ardin was curious, but just as elated as I.

He leaned on the door jamb, hand on his forehead, "What purpose does this room hold now?"

"I don't know nor do I care."

The door had vanished as always. I came out of the room. Thanos collected his scythe as it left the

Eulogy

door.

"What are you doing? I've got ghosts to attend to."

Fearless and smug, I replied, "Well, you will be happy to know that Marchosias became breakfast for my dragon this fine morning. I needed the assistance of our scythe to open the portal. It will not happen again, Thanos."

"I should hope not. I've got more important things to attend to than the murder of annoyances and the *protection* of relics." His voice was uncharacteristically high pitched at the mockery.

"Thanos, the time is coming near to our purpose of this army. Would you be willing to help us?"

"My purpose is not your purpose, Centurion of Time," like mist, he smoked away, scythe in hand.

"There's a black sheep in every family, I supposed. What a dysfunctional one we are," Ardin scoffed with a slight laugh.

We ascended the stairwell again. Our light-heartedness came to an abrupt standstill as a commotion exploded on the deck.

"Help him, someone," one of the new recruits voiced.

A.R. Perkins

I rushed to Gad, "It will be okay! What's wrong?

"Banshees, by God the screams!" holding his ears with both palms. His eyes were blood shot from a sound no one else could hear. He, then relieved from his cringing fetal state, stood up and released his ears.

"All the evil not here on earth was screaming terrified shrills inside my head."

"What did they say?" I was curious as to what brought this on all of a sudden.

"You will not kill him. We will reign forever! I know what the future holds and you are all DEAD!"

"Marchosias," I was again made the fuel behind a fire that could not be extinguished.

"We must leave this place, NOW! They are going to hunt us and we cannot allow this evil amongst the innocent of Jerusalem. Gather everything; we must head to Rome, but not by sea. No, on second thought, leave it all. Only take the gold and the transports. We must travel light with the speed of the wind," I was panicking. No key to lead me, the angst took over in choppy commands.

"What of the senators, Centurion?" A

Eulogy

responsible question the only one that kept me sane when I was completely lost, my dear friend, Gad.

"Yes, um . . . the Senators and the army, have they been fed?"

"Yes, sir," Eryx and Aristos chimed.

"Then, they must come too, or all will be lost. Get them off the boat; their steeds will be as our steeds."

"Without Thanos, how will this be?"

"We must *bother* him again then I suppose."

"Do you think that wise, he will not help us, if we bother him unnecessarily again?" Ardin was starting to get on my nerves with this nonsense, even without Thanos here; he wanted to whine about his existence.

"*Thanos,*" I mind ordered as always and before with thought and stern ordering of word. I knew it would work, it had to. The door may be used as a portal, but my power had more pull to him than anything else. Eyes glowing red flame before he solidified from grey and green smoke, staring at me all the while.

"Listen! Before you even start, I have a massive undertaking I must request of you. I know, you have been punished for your wicked deed against the Almighty, but perhaps, this one act could redeem you from your punishment."

"That's what you don't understand, Centurion. I have come to accept the fact that I will never see my family again. I enjoy being alone."

"You do not seem to understand the importance of our mission, Thanos. Without completing this, you will have no purpose. There will be no souls to ferry to the afterlife. All will die and only go to one place. There will be no prayers or retribution for those who have passed. Without a destination point, your purpose will cease to exist, and therefore, so will you."

He scoffed at me and burned a hole through me with his eyes again, "Do you really think that I care whether or not I even exist? *You* took *everything* from me. I would rather remain a transforming apparition then to assist you in your quest. That is why, even knowing the protection of John's soul, I attempted to pull it from him. Yes, like Gad, I have the gift of perception as well. I am just not as vocal about it as he is."

"We *need* your help, Thanos. Without your

Eulogy

gifts, we cannot change the steeds into dragons; we cannot defeat Nero . . . *please, Thanos, I'm begging you!*"

Thanos laughed loudly and darkly at my pain, "Thank you, you have given me the greatest gift. The great Centurion of Time is begging me, his servant for assistance."

He laughed all the more, I looked at him, mouth opened, completely confused and shocked at his vendetta against me.

"You cannot control me, Centurion," laughing again.

Is this how God must feel; was it such a mistake to give free wills to mankind as it was for me to give immortality to this vile creature of bones? My mental growl was hard to hide from him as my eyes clenched tight, my teeth ground slivers on my tongue. My fists reacted simultaneously. Then recognizing each other's human emotions had not escaped our immortality, I collected my sanity. I ran the idea through my mind and wished to speak the words to banish him forever, but my pride was not the quest here.

I attempted one more thing, *"Go to the stable."*

A.R. Perkins

Thanos disappeared. Ardin and I ran to the stable and, behold, he was there! The entire Equestrians' steeds were within. The room had transformed in enormity as usual.

"Touch all the steeds."

He did so as I and Ardin slid beside him and did so as he did so; all the transfers of power were complete, and the steeds were no longer stallions, but beasts.

"What happened?"

He woke from his trance just before, *"Return to Purgatory"* was uttered. Regardless of his obstinacy, without a free flowing energy source to defy my will, he was easily controlled. He thought he was his own master, but all that remained was an empty hull of bones.

"He seized the dragon and bound him for a thousand years." — Revelation 20:2

Broken

"Would you *please* explain to me why I cannot get any help around here? I have to dress myself, bathe myself, I even have to make my own disastrous midnight snacks." Nero, dressed in a bright orange lace-frilled toga, hair a mess, sleep still crusted in his eyes, was yelling at Seneca in the throne room. "I know I need to leave this place. My guards and maid servants have abandoned me. I just don't know how to take care of myself!"

"Perhaps you are right sire, but where would you go that no one would be able to find you?"

Seneca was secretly pleased at this, though he portrayed the part of his most trusted friend.

"I don't know. I did not unpack from my voyage to Ostia. No one obeyed me on that ship either. I pled with them to show mercy onto me and forgive me for my selfish acts. My dear Epaphroditos fought them off while I got away. I wonder if he ever made it back."

"He did sire, but he is in the hospital from his wounds," Seneca laughed quietly as he coughed.

"O, well, he will be fine and ready to be at my

Eulogy

side in no time.   For now, I must plan an exit strategy."

"He is due to be out of the hospital tomorrow."

"Send my traveling coach to pick him up then. He will ride in privacy and style." Nero raised his mighty chins as he said this.

Seneca thought a bit about that and replied, "Do you think that wise, sire, with all the threats against your life?"

Nero cringe his regal stature, "Um . . . perhaps you're right. Send your coach instead, Seneca."

"Yes sire." Seneca bowed out, retreating to give the order.

I hated these visions.   How am I supposed to know where this man will be from one minute to the next?   I had an inner monologue of his inner monologue. I was not too enthused about the fact that I had access to the mind of Belial.

Neither he nor I knew who he was until Marchosias told him and I started receiving these visions.   Understandably, the snake must be disguised so the he would not fear being trodden upon. His actions though could not be masked for long. The personality of a demon, even slight as it may be, would prove its true identity.

"Are you back?"

Ardin had noticed my staring state, "Hm?"

"Have you returned from whatever fantasy world you were in?"

"O, yes Ardin, sorry."

"What is happening anyway, leader, I feel left in the dark most of the time."

I told him about my new gifts and apologized to him about leaving him out of the loop. We had to act quickly. Now that the newly changed had transportation, I had to know they could be trusted. The senators would fly with Gad, Ardin, and I, the soldiers brought their own means that Thanos reluctantly changed. We gathered all the soldiers and tethered the dragons together. We waited for sunset and started the flight above the clouds.

'Go to our meadow, Marcellus. We must strategize.'

The multitude smoothly disembarked. As their paws touched, each altered in appearance to hooves, right on up to their manes. The magic shook from them as they whinnied and collected their new frames. No words were spoken. Moonshine,

Eulogy

Marcellus, and Brutus remained as their former selves. Pax came to greet us.

"The maidens are still safe, my liege," his hand floated over his belly as he bowed to me.

"Thank you, as always for your diligence, Pax. How are things?"

Chin in an upward position, "Very well, sire, I am surviving on the animals as you had requested, though it is rather difficult. I enjoy the fact that I do not age. I saw myself in the pool's reflection the other day. I know it has been many years that I have remained here on my task."

"I am content for you, Pax. We, on the other hand, have been scrambling on our own purpose. May we join you in your cabin?"

"Yes sire, o, yes, please excuse my lack of hospitality. I cannot guarantee that there will be enough space for all of you though."

"Well then, do you have chairs?"

"Yes, actually, I build them in my spare time; it is a hobby of mine. I have many, many chairs."

"WONDERFUL! Bring them out here! Make a bon fire and we will have a fireside chat."

Pax flitted with the chairs, Ardin zipped after

firewood, and Brutus lit the fire. The three of us were comfortable with an old rotting log Ardin found on his firewood venture.

I empathized to address any concerns there may be with the transition process.

"Please, be assured that this change was meant to suit your purpose and not to harm you. You must be careful when hunting. You must hunt only at night and red is the only hue you may consume. The process is irreversible and discretion amongst the mortals is *vital*. Know this; our target has many spies. He is linked to the underworld by the very souls of man. We may have to seek out others to fulfill this purpose, but the revelation must be after this change. It is a necessary evil in order to fulfill our purpose and keep our secrecy.

"There is only One who now owns your souls and has replaced it with these endowments. He requests a simple service from you in order to give you peace. We are the Soldiers of God. Many of you may find that you have other talents along the way."

I waved my hand at Moonshine and Gad. She pointed towards the clearing, away from the

Eulogy

audience, and expelled her electricity. The men were astounded. Gad looked at her and she smiled as he embellished praises on her without a word uttered. Brutus looked at her communicating silently. Her ivory cheekbones blushed- two light pink rose blossoms.

"We have fought the darkness straight out of Hades; we have protected sacred relics from its very claws; we have sliced them to crow feed, burnt them to ash, and crumbled them to rumble. Our monsters are trusted friends that we communicate with through the mind. With you on our side, soldiers from one life will be unstoppable war weapons in this one. Fulfill your task and our life-forces will be free."

The soldiers' eyes glistened and their shoulders stood a bit higher.

Piso spoke first, "Well, can you enlighten us on any dealings you have had in these matters?"

I responded as honestly as I could, "I know that he is thinking about fleeing, but I cannot pin point the destination. We must act as quickly as possible, for all will be lost if he gathers up enough nerve to follow the soothsayer's advice."

"I understand all this," he waved his hand in aggravation. "Believe me; I want him off the throne more so than any other man here."

'Are you sure about that?'

This ran through me.

Gad whispered to me, "The only reason he wants him gone is for his own succession. That is what this whole coup is about."

"Can we trust them to assist in *our* purpose?"

"O, yes, they will fulfill their vow! We must hope that all goes well. They do not realize, what will be regardless of what you have told them. Piso still believes he will be emperor after Nero's death. He will be sorely mistaken."

"Why?"

"Because, there can only be one man to rule the entire world when the Antichrist is destroyed."

I leaned away from him, awakened by this epiphany.

"So what happens when we succeed?"

Gad replied, "The obvious, of course, our bodies will join our life-forces."

"And . . . what will happen to everyone else?"

"Well, I suppose we will find that out when that

Eulogy

time comes. We are not going to be here so, what does it matter?"

This was very uncharacteristic of Gad. I was curious and his powers should be attuned to the foreshadowing circumstances. This mutated my curiosity to confusion. The soldier mumbled amongst themselves around the bon-fire. Long ago, we may have shared legends and a skewer of wild boar. I only sat and took in the commotion, as a shadow lies before the sun. We were getting nowhere, but I couldn't be angry. They were waiting on me . . . patiently. All but Piso, he waited for me to continue the conversation we were having, staring through me. I did not reciprocate. It was only the others that enjoyed the down time. Piso was anxious to act. But, it was late and Nero was sleeping. If he dreamed, I was not privy to the scene. My experience had taught me not to travel blindly.

I continued to feel his eyes on me as I stared into the fire. My thoughts were my own until the moon shone high in the sky. The same light pierced through the sheer curtains at the palace. Nero woke gasping and jolting straight up.

A.R. Perkins

I cannot release those words from my mind. 'Why do you fear the end, Belial? The one way that you could not fail to reign again is to commit the sin upon yourself.' Argh! I love this life; I do not want it to end. I will call upon the guards, yes; they will protect me from those who seek to destroy me.

"Guards," Nero called.

No one answered.

"Useless, they must be asleep outside the chamber. *I WILL HAVE THEIR HEADS!*"

He forced open the enormous marble door, surprised at the strength his frustration relented. "WAKE U. . ." no one heard his rant.

Standing there, mouth gaped; Nero twiddled his fingers against the door. He then turn and grasped his lips, trying to pull them off from the accumulation of fear, anger, and worry.

'Tonight, I must get out of here.'

Images blipped across his mind's eye randomly. Port Ostia, Parthia, kneeling humbly to the Galanians for safe passage to Egypt, then he remembered the soldiers from the voyage past, and he felt embarrassment in the realization of their

Eulogy

gossip.

'I will write my acquaintances and find salvation with them.'

So I witnessed as he wrote several letters and ordered a sleeping page-boy to deliver them. He waited impatiently on his bed, jostling his knee up and down with his foot until the moon had moved inches across the sky.

He then went back to the page-boys quarters and woke him, yelling *"YOU WORTHLESS CHILD, DID YOU SEND THE DISPATCHES?"*

Groggy and frightened, he stuttered, "Y-y-yes, your majesty. I have been resting for quite some time." It was two in the morning now, and Nero left in a fury to the homes the messages were sent. He pounded on their doors. He did not wait long for an answer before he barged in, only to find they were gone.

I felt the panic striking his heart and the sorrow in his mind. He ran to the Coliseum, and for begged the gladiators to put him to death. The head master held them locked in the basement cells. Though slightly awake, he feared trickery and punishment for obliging his request and declined.

A.R. Perkins

Nero left in a huff, mumbling, "Have I neither friend nor foe?"

The fear of the unknown was driving him mad. The goal transpired before me.

"No!"

I attempted to mind order him as if he were one of my own, then shuddered at that thought. He ran toward the Tiber and hesitated minutes before. The thought of sucking water into his lungs paralyzed his limbs.

"There must be someone that can help me, whether I order them as friend or slave!"

He returned to the palace and waited for morning. The habits of the soldiers reminded them of my odd staring position. They were talking amongst themselves for hours while I remained comatose, experiencing the mind's eye of Nero's actions.

Piso sighed and looked at me frustrated.

I returned his gaze, "What?"

"Are you aware, centurion that we have sat here all night without a single battle plan from you? We were in awe of your powers, but it seems that you put on a pretty show, with no results. We paid you

Eulogy

a high price, and for what?"

I, being totally oblivious of the time, did not understand his frustration with me. Dawn was approaching.

"Again Piso, part of my talents, are that I can view the mind of the one we seek. We must act as soon as possible, for he knows of the conspiracy . . ."

Interrupting, "But, how . . ?"

I shook my hand at him, "Don't worry about the how, I need to know the when. Right now, he is at the palace, but he is planning on fleeing. I need to pin point where he *will* be."

"Just how can I trust the fact that you are doing what you say you are doing? How do I know that you are not completely insane? I am not impressed. Come on men!"

I stood up, raced to his shoulder, pushing him to return to his seat.

"After all this, you still don't believe?"

The men as well returned to their chairs, their seats did not travel far before my distraction. They knew I had to say something to him to make them stay.

A.R. Perkins

"I do not care if he dies from other means, as long as he is dead."

"So," I said, "Therein lays the problem. You cannot trust that I will assist you in your quest for power, and I cannot trust you to assist in the salvation of the world. As I have said, the power is given to us for a purpose; you only do this to fulfill the purpose of your own succession."

"How did you . . ?"

"I told you, we have talents of our own. Now unless you wish to live a life of immortality and murder, constantly on your conscience, never to be released, or you can help us and live forever in paradise."

This only angered him and did not go the way I wished. He did not do well with ultimatums and I was beginning to understand him all the more from this conversation. What would I do with him afterwards? Perhaps the room for Marchosias would be the appropriate cell for him.

Dawn was nigh and the visions began again: flipping like a buzzing bee from flower to flower, Nero's mind constantly changing and nowhere seemed distinct. Piso sighed again at me.

Eulogy

"Let's go men," I heard this echo in the back of my mind. The vision ended as I saw a blinding light out of the corner of my eye. I awoke to realty.

"I wondered when you were going to show up. I have tried everything, Gabriel, but they will not believe. Their motivations are not our own."

"I know. I apologize. I was postponed giving revelations to a certain prophet."

"The elevation of my power is not helping. Marchosias told him everything, and now he is deceiving only as a demon can do. I cannot pin where he will be so that the quest can be accomplished."

"I know everything. Marchosias' power was transferred to me when your beast devoured him. He resides on a plane, not living or dead. The brimstone within Marcellus consumed even his spirit."

Gad confused at this, asked, "Then how was he able to scream inside my head?"

"That was not Marchosias, the voice sounded like his and portrayed itself as his words, with his gifts, but it was an illusion transmitted from the kings of Hell."

A.R. Perkins

The soldiers, including Piso, were completely convinced now that Gabriel had arrived. They had never seen anything like him in all their days.

"I know where Belial will be, even if he does not know himself. The fallen Throne, who had used the omniscience of God for the purpose of evil, now comes full circle to its rightful place." He bowed to me, "For this, I commend you. Jesus was right about you. To fulfill your vow and release your souls, find haven."

Then, he was gone. A trumpet sounded at his disappearance.

I was glad that he had found peace with me. Everything though still seemed a deep seeded rage with in me regarding the circumstances leading to this hour. The load was a bit lighter, but how could one forgive and forget when I still lived it? I remained untrusting. Just like Marchosias, Gabriel spoke in riddles. The only way I could truly find peace or haven as he so put it, was to kill this devil in sheep's clothing: not the other way around.

After thinking on this and continuing to vent internally, still entranced, "Well now what are we supposed to do? That did not help at all!"

Eulogy

"Centurion," Ardin looked at me, face to face, from his former passenger position, "one of the soldiers just told us the answer to that question."

"Out with it then, why will no one let me in the loop on this?"

"Centurion, he was speaking directly to you, but you did not acknowledge him."

O! The consequences of stress! Gabriel should have given me two minds to match with my two eyes and two ears. Maybe that will be the next upgrade if this fails, then I could truly look like a freak.

I laughed out loud at my own thoughts, which of course, caused odd looks in my direction.

"So?"

The soldier aggravated, "I *said* . . . Haven is a childhood friend of Nero's who lives four miles outside of Rome. He will not go unprotected though and he will go in disguise. We are not the only Romans that would want him dead."

"I thought his mother was exiled."

"Yes, she was exiled from the palace; she stayed with her wet nurse in that villa, while she attempted to win the hearts of the Senate, hoping the emperor would allow her return. Agrippa, remained friends with Haven's mother and allowed her into the palace as her hand maiden. She left the home to Haven, and he moved there when he became of age."

"You know this place?"

"Yes, it is a villa, high on a mountainside."

When the sun was setting, we had finally reached the time of the end.

"We must leave, by air, now!"

"How do we get the steeds into the air?" Piso queried.

"Mount them and get them up to speed, if they do not change when we take flight, I will change them myself."

The farm boy had disappeared. I had finally come into my own. I needed help from the ethereal, but how could I possibly be expected to succeed as a former mortal? I was shooting into the dark, and faith could only take me so far. Was it even possible for me to succeed in this responsibility?

The soldiers hoisted into their saddles confidently and settled the stallions with their reins. They seemed impatient to leave after being dormant

Eulogy

of action for over a day. Slowly, each from rank to lesser rank formed a v-formation. One by one, they began to trot, then gallop, then full force; they ran as if their hamstrings would burst. They would not change on their own.

'Away, Marcellus, order the others!'

He took flight and the others followed, the steeds began to transform. Their wings outstretched, catching the wind they created from their speed. I and Marcellus flew in front, Brutus and Ardin took the right and Moonshine flew at the rear to the left, Therius was to the rear and the right flank. Even in this, I held a protective mind set. Four was not nearly enough, of course, but I hoped experience would win out, regardless of number.

I felt out the magic of the process, still unsure of the will that was behind the power. High above the clouds, we flew the short distance, still anxious to make it in time before I received another vision that would seal Nero's fate. I became content in the absence of their nuisance.

"Whoa! What was that?" Brutus' wings crumbled in towards his body. He fell a few feet, then righted himself. Gad looked toward him as did the others. The others' mounts fell too, as the diversion hit them with the same blast. They returned to formation. Marcellus shared his sight with me as he saw it within the others' minds. I felt the fear he felt, as they experienced it. I returned the fear with confusion.

'Keep the pace but fall to the rear, Marcellus.'

He obeyed, and the invisible force returned.

The equestrians and the senators dominoed into each other as they lost control; Marcellus rushed to one's aid as he flew underneath his belly and pushed him upward. The rest continued to fall, as Moonshine, Brutus, and other unscathed went to save as many as they could. Only few could be righted at a time, and many others continued to hurl to the ground. Blast after blast, over and over, the force caused the salvaged to lose control.

"Gad, what is this?" He did not respond, and only looked at me with distress.

"Look!" Gad pointed skyward. He was receptive of the new threat, but not the former. I dared not conclude why. Balls of every rung of the rainbow began to fall from above the hazing atmosphere. I shut my eyes to brace for the impact.

Eulogy

Instead, there was a round of blood boiling screams. Flitting, my eyes blazed to find the source: leather faced and winged, feathers matching the fireballs' tint, long gangly fingers crept towards my face. My forearm stressed for the impact, as Marcellus hurled his muzzle upward to bat him away. There was not enough time to release his jaws grasp to devour the threat. I lost the sense of the others as the small human salvation instinct took over. Marcellus' action woke me from this state, as I began to notice the dexterity in art before me. The many fallen stars attacked as the winds' force continued, but the newly changed learned to avert the enemy as they swooped around them in flickers.

This was a diversion from our mission, and more than just an annoyance. Now I was angry. I did not want to *have to feel* the vulnerability of these visions *anymore*! Nero would continue to kill, regardless of this conspiracy, simply because he could. I knew where he would be and I had to be there, then, not years from now. I *had* to be done with this.

Just when it seemed the dragons were catching on to diverting the gusts and about to devour the miniature transformed stars, I heard thunderous roars from beneath me. A giant red dragon, larger than Brutus, rushed as a bull towards Ardin. Behind him: winged green eels with razor sharp teeth, manta rays fueled by their stinger's electricity, ebony winged mustangs fashioning flames for manes and tails, wyverns, harpies, winged goblins, specters of fog, smoke and dust: a literal army of flight.

Therius was finally able to pull alongside the attackers and began using his talents at the creatures as they rushed towards us. He could not fend them all off though as we were defiantly outnumbered.

I prayed the phoenixes would return. Marcellus heard my prayers and hoped for it too. I looked around as best I could for them to come to our aid amidst the heavenly battle. No aiding flames flew in site.

The hummingbird-like motion continued from the recruits. Their aversions led them into traps of the reinforcements. I heard the sound of diamond scraping stone as many were ripped from their mounts and hurled to the inevitability below. Their loyal steeds attempted to dive-bomb to their rescue

Eulogy

only to be paralyzed but the bolts the rays equipped. The equestrians were salvaged, while three-quarters of the soldiers fell. I wanted to fly down to them and retrieve them and pick their bodies up, but their steeds acquired the ability to die as they plummeted, motionless to the earth. Dust blew up from the points of propulsion, denting the land like a cannon thud.

They fought a wondrous fight, I would retrieve the soldiers when this nightmare relinquished. I was correct when I thought experience would win out, the few that remained sat with us on our saddles. The conspiracy had dwindled and the sin to curse them for the greater good became naught.

The army of evil rushed towards us as the others were no longer a threat. I saw the future of fear flash into Marcellus' mind. I saw us falling as well as the great red dragon rider thrust his great chest into him, while the others were overtaken.

In that moment, I was then blinded by a violet light. The gaily winds ceased, the impish beings covered their eyes with their leathered wings and fell away from their flight in our direction. The mantas, harpies, and specters evaporated mid-rush and became one with the clouds. One remained and the vision was still a near reality.

Raphael barreled towards the rider and removed him from his mount. His beast paused midflight and followed its master. Raphael turned to me, wings gracefully oscillating to uplift his body.

"Be gone, Asmodai, never unearth again!" Asmodai had been hurled, full force into the sea.

"Now, onto your quest, centurion, I will find and heal the others. They will meet you at Haven's villa."

His wings collapsed around him as he ventured toward his promise.

Marcellus continued to fly as I was rendered helpless again.

"You there, dig me a grave. I have no reason to live. I cannot live with this knowledge and shame."

Nero had judged and killed as though he were a jealous god. Now, knowing his impending fate, he ordered his companions to murder him.

"We have to hurry!"

"No, you, there . . ." Nero pointed, "I cannot do this; you will take my place in the grave. Kill yourself so that I can see how it is done."

CCCXLII

Eulogy

"No, sire, I have a family. I will not do your bidding simply to save your life, or is it simply for your own amusement?"

Nero opened his mouth to speak, but the equestrians made their approach. Who could have known, Raphael's gifts would be so potent? The elixir rejuvenated the steeds with fervor. They arrived far before Marcellus could cut through the clouds to the destination below us.

"Hark, now strikes on my ear the trampling of swift-footed coursers! Epaphroditos, my faithful servant, get the dagger!"

"Gladly sire."

The vision was no more and was plainly before me. Marcellus landed, I leaped off his back. But it was too late. Epaphroditos held Nero's hand as he forced the dagger into his throat.

"NOOOO," I cried. I knew the inevitable had come and past me by.

Was this a test? Was this self-made god not the anti-Christ? I fell to my knees in front of the bleeding corpse. The spear lay in my hands before me. Gabriel flashed to the left of me. I looked at him and then to the blood seeping into the sand.

A.R. Perkins

"The unicorn's neck has broken. The horn is now the grip of the Son of God's sword. He will yield it when He returns. The key to Hell has been buried on the earth at Armageddon. The beast shall rise from whence and start his terror. Their beast will be as your beasts. Marcus will roam free. Oriana is now a servant of the fallen, though flames no longer singe her brilliant hair."

At that, I leaped to his throat with the spear. He disappeared. The point broke off the spear and fell to the ground where he once stood.

I shouted to the air. "NEVER COME TO ME AGAIN. WHAT PURPOSE SHOULD I HAVE FOR YOU NOW?"

A red and black flash came before me. My eyes glared at them with the same goal of vengeance in mind. I started at them as well. The white haired man in the red robe held out his palm and stopped my movement. He looked at me and spoke in my mind.

'I am Metatron and this is Azrael. We have decided to allow your lovely to live, but you must fulfill your purpose.'

"Gabriel said she would be as the un-dead of

Eulogy

Thanos' charge, she would regret and want to die."

'*Her body may not lie in the ground but her soul is. Once reborn she will have no memory of the life with you. If I erase her name, it will be recycled and God has elected to show you mercy. He will create a body as hers was once, her soul will live within. This is your second chance. You will have to wait for her, but you will see her once again. You have favor with God though you could not fulfill your purpose today.*"

"How will I know where she is?"

'*Your lives will be intertwined in purpose.*'

"How will I know when the end is near again?"

'*We do not even know.*

List of Characters

Army of God

Centurion	Leader of the cursed
Ardin (Leander)	friend of Centurion, leader of Free Masons
Thanos (Petronius)	Guard of Christ's tomb, Reaper of Souls
Gad, Issachar, Matthias	Nailed Christ to the cross.
Peregrine	Captain of Fidelis Donec Terminus
Aristos & Atalo	Brothers of war and fire, protégés of Ardin
Nen	Power of water, charged with protection of scrolls & scribes
Therius & Nuri	Brothers of air and protection
Bedros	telekinesis of rock
Eryx	Stone hands

List of Characters

Angels

Gabriel	Hand of the end of the world
Michael	Leader of all angels
Raphael	Healer
Urial	Angel of God's Light
Cassiel	Angel of pure love, Gabriel's protégé
Ramiel	Author of Zohar, a book containing all the secrets of Heaven, given the Adam & Eve and left in Eden

List of Characters

Demons

Belial	King of the Northern part of Hell
Chimirias	Colonel of the written word
Marbus	Healer
Vesper	King of the Southern part of Hell
Marchosias	Knowledge of the Future

Here I repose in mire and shame;
Cursed to walk the world: I roam
The spear of destiny bears my name
I pierced the side and broke no bone.

A utilitarian vagabond, meant to lead
A legion that shares my fate
The supply is based upon the need
The wicked world I've grown to hate

People are blessed with forgiveness
I lost that privilege long ago
But they see their life as frivolous
And are apathetic to the value of their soul

Spear in hand; a beat less heart;
"Death": my general at my side
Though our lives seem worlds apart
My objective is to shape the fate of mankind

Until the insane become the sane
And void and flame become sublime
Until the end, I will remain
Frozen forever in time